Given In Honor of

John F. Helgeson

By
Diane H. Byerly

D1443962

A Matter of Abuse

John Helgeson

Eloquent Books

Eloquent Books
An imprint of Strategic Book Group
P.O. Box 333
Durham CT 06422
www.StrategicBookGroup.com

ISBN: 978-1-60860-914-7

Printed in the United States of America

Dedicated

To my wife and daughters

Chapter 1

The Official Story

This is the official story of the incident as pieced together from written reports, interviews with staff and interested parties, as well as informal channels of communication. The narrative was written anonymously by a member of the staff known to have writing skills.

On the night of May 1, about eight-thirty p.m., while trying to put her eight-year-old daughter Melissa to bed, Mrs. Angela Gunnarsen (nee Bonicelli) hit her daughter in the face repeatedly when Melissa became defiant and refused to go to sleep. Though the child became passive and started crying out to her mother to stop hitting her, Mrs. Gunnarsen continued to hit the child harder and harder for a period of fifteen minutes. As a result, one of Melissa's eyes was partially closed and turned black and blue. Elsewise on the child's face were inflicted scars, bruises and swellings.

Melissa's father, Andrew Gunnarsen, was not in the house at the time. He is a businessman, who was out on assigned duties commensurate with his occupation. There is no evidence Mr. Gunnarsen had any knowledge of his wife's actions in regard to their daughter until the next morning (see subsequent paragraphs for further information about the father's belated obtaining of such knowledge). Mr. Gunnarsen did not return home until close to eleven p.m. By that time, his wife had retired to her bed and his daughter was sleeping.

A second daughter Nicole, age eleven, was also preparing for bed at the time of the incident. Though she occupies a different room than Melissa, she heard Melissa screaming and ran to her sister's room. She saw her mother beating Melissa as reported above. What she saw caught her so off guard that for several moments all she could do was watch. This was interrupted when Melissa seeing her sister Nicole present, screamed out to Nicole for help. Nicole at that point yelled at her mother to stop. Nicole continued to yell for some five minutes. When this did not stop the beatings, Nicole threw herself at her mother and physically intervened, grabbing her mother's hands, courageously placing herself in between her mother and sister.

This action apparently startled Mrs. Gunnarsen and as a result she stopped beating Melissa. Mrs. Gunnarsen muttered an obscenity and sat down on the bed. She immediately hugged both of her children and assured them she did love them both and would never do anything to hurt either of them. The two girls cried and mother joined in. They sat and cried and hugged for about a half-hour. Subsequently, Mrs. Gunnarsen and Nicole left the room. Melissa went to sleep. Nicole went to her own bed. Mrs. Gunnarsen withdrew to the family room to watch TV for about another half-hour and then went to bed.

Upon returning home, Mr. Gunnarsen watched the eleven-p.m. news and read the daily newspaper for a short while before proceeding to bed himself. Mr. Gunnarsen does not leave for work until nine a.m. because of his regular evening hours out of the house. Consequently, he is the last person to arise in the morning. Mrs. Gunnarsen arises at six a.m. to prepare the children for school, Nicole being in the sixth grade and Melissa in the third. Mr. Gunnarsen usually awakens just prior to the children's departure, often seeing them out the door.

On the morning of May 2, the usual schedule was followed by all concerned. As the children were going out the door and Mrs. Gunnarsen was in the kitchen starting to prepare breakfast for her husband before he went to work, Melissa stopped, turned to her father and said, "Daddy, Mommy hurt me badly last night."

She pointed to her eye, which was still black and blue, and to her face, which exhibited signs of puffiness. Before her father could respond, she quickly exited the house and went to school. Andrew Gunnarsen moved into the kitchen, sat down for his breakfast, turned to his wife and said, "Melissa says you hurt her last night, and her face looks a mess. What the hell is going on?"

Mr. Gunnarsen reports his wife turned pale at the question and sat rather artificially in her chair at the kitchen table. She started to cry. "Angela, what happened last night?" Mr. Gunnarsen said he asked his wife.

"She would not go to bed for me last night and so I hit her. But I couldn't stop hitting her. I couldn't stop hitting her until Nicole grabbed me and actually put herself in between me and Melissa. I didn't mean to; I didn't plan to. It just happened. You know how difficult Melissa can be, especially at bedtime. I guess I was just impatient, angry and I couldn't take it any longer. So I hit her, I hit her, I hit her!"

Mrs. Gunnarsen reports her husband Andrew looked at her in shock and in askance. "I thought I knew you better. How could you do such a thing?"

Her reply was to indicate that Melissa was a difficult child as even he knew and finally her patience broke. She could not take it any longer and just could not control her anger against Melissa. She knew it was wrong, but she was unable to stop.

She went on to suggest that she might need professional counseling and that he might have to watch the children for a while lest she repeat this action. He promised he would be home early that night, canceling any evening meetings and assuring her he would put the children to bed that night. She was also to call him at work several times during the day and let him know how she was doing. Such was the gist of their conversation.

He prepared for work and left at the customary time. Approximately an hour and a half later, while Mrs. Gunnarsen was at home cleaning the house, she received a phone call from the school nurse. The school nurse mentioned what she saw in Melissa's face and indicated that Mrs. Gunnarsen should get some help if there was a problem. She further stated that since this was a first-time incident, she did not foresee any other actions being taken by the school or appropriate authorities.

The principal of the school, Mr. Rizzick, had also seen Melissa's face that morning, as he had made it a policy to greet all the children on their arrival at school. He did not talk to the school nurse. Rather, after greeting all the children, he walked into his office and immediately called the state child-abuse hotline. He reported what he saw to the appropriate state authorities and provided names, addresses, phone numbers and other information he had available concerning the parents as well as the children.

Social workers Ann Brown and Jolene Raycox were assigned to the case. Under state procedures, they were to go to the house of the parents that day and interview them first (if possible) before the children arrived home. The children would be interviewed subsequently and privately. Following the interview, the social workers would report back to their immediate superior, the case manager. The threesome would proceed to decide on what would be the next step in the case. The possibilities ranged from the extremes of dismissing the case out of hand if nothing was perceived to have transpired to removing the children form the situation if the situation was perceived as imminently dangerous to the welfare of the children. Other than removing the children (if something was perceived to have happened), various possible actions could be taken. The social workers and the case manager had widespread flexibility in working out a plan of action depending on the situation itself.

At precisely 2:02 p.m., social workers Ann Brown and Jolene Raycox knocked on the door of the house of Angela and Andrew Gunnarsen. Mrs. Gunnarsen answered the door. She was informed that they were social workers for the state Children's Affairs Division. They were there to investigate a possible child-abuse situation. They needed to talk to Mrs.

Gunnarsen, her husband, and her children. Mrs. Gunnarsen was hesitant about admitting them until they informed her that if she did not cooperate voluntarily, they had the authority to call the police and force entry, have her arrested on the spot and brought in for questioning. Also, refusal to cooperate under state laws was an automatic admission of guilt. Children's safety required assuming the children must be protected at all costs and thus parents must be assumed to be abusers.

Upon hearing this litany, Mrs. Gunnarsen let the social workers into the house. The house was clean, perhaps compulsively so was the impression of Ann Brown. Compulsiveness would go far in explaining Mrs. Gunnarsen's abusing her child. A compulsive parent would be too demanding of a child and quick to strike out and eventually abuse the child when the child did not meet up to the compulsive's expectations.

Sitting in the living room with Mrs. Gunnarsen, the social workers took turns questioning her about the previous evening's events. Using tested procedures they alternated between threats and subtle cajoling. They could be judge or cop one moment and friend and confidante the next. Mrs. Gunnarsen quickly confessed to having hit Melissa, but she denied it was abusive. She insisted it was for the moment and that the child did not exhibit any significant facial characteristics that would demonstrate abuse.

Mrs. Gunnarsen was extremely nervous during this interview, unable to remain seated for more than a few moments, her right foot shaking continually, her right hand combing her hair almost non-stop. Her talk was fast but staccato. Her left hand seemed to gesture in contradiction to her words, felt both Brown and Raycox. Her eyes could not look directly at either Brown or Raycox.

The more they talked the more the social workers became convinced Mrs. Gunnarsen had indeed abused the child. At this point they were unsure of the husband's role in all of this, even though she told them her husband had not been home at the time of the incident as he had been working. Such statements are under regulation guidelines to be treated with skepticism, since both parents are assumed to be either involved in the act or one parent consciously or unconsciously gives the other parent permission to abuse the child. It would be up to the Gunnarsens to prove that Andrew Gunnarsen was not also abusing the child.

When the children arrived home from school, they were brought face to face with the social workers. They had to be told their regular schedules, for the day would be set aside. The parents had them both in dance, and this was their normal dance day. Obviously that had to be cancelled in order for the social workers to ascertain the truth of the situation and protect the children if necessary from further abuse. The children would also need to be told why the social workers were present.

Ann Brown insisted on the girls calling her Ann, feeling that would help ease their tension. She wanted to be their friend, someone they could talk to one on one and not be afraid to talk to. When she did explain whey she and Jolene Raycox were in the house, Melissa started to scream and run throughout the house, finally coming to rest in her mother's lap and saying, "No, no, no!" She turned to the social workers and added, "I won't let you take my mother away."

Having been through this scene before, Brown told Melissa that she was there to help Melissa and Nicole and to help her mother too. She did not want to take her mother away; she wanted to help everybody.

This was of course a slight prevarication. Social workers in child-abuse situations may very well have to require the separation of parent and child, but that is not to be dealt with unless it actually happens. Telling the child that could happen (at least hypothetically, though often actually, in such actions) leads the child to assume it will happen. Once the child makes that assumption, the child can be very difficult to deal with. The child may refuse to speak up; the child may be too emotionally distraught by the possibility of losing the parent as to be unable to speak; and in a few specific situations, the child may want the parent out of the picture and is more than willing to exaggerate the truth or make up stories if that will remove the parent.

Melissa, Mrs. Gunnarsen had said, was medically certified as hyperactive. Ann Brown had no background in the field of hyperactivity, but Jolene Raycox did. Ann Brown was the point person, the leader of the team, but Jolene Raycox was the medically, psychologically trained partner who could make sense out of such claims. Mrs. Gunnarsen did provide medical records to the team certifying that Melissa was indeed hyperactive.

As a hyperactive child, Melissa would require more discipline, more control. Specifically, the doctors had agreed that in Melissa's case, corporeal punishment would be necessary at times, simply to focus her attention. Despite this in writing, Ann Brown was uneasy about corporeal punishment; it could too easily be used as an excuse for abusive behavior by the parent. She had seen it before, and it appeared to her as if she were seeing it again.

On the other hand, Jolene Raycox had worked with hyperactive children before and knew whereof the doctors spoke. She also realized that raising such a child would and could be difficult. Additionally, if the child was medicated, that made the situation more complex. Certain types of medicines for hyperactive children were known to provoke bizarre, occasionally paranoid symptoms in some children. If such symptoms persisted, the child would be almost impossible to control by anybody, least of all a frustrated parent trying to put a medically unwilling child to bed.

Melissa's behavior to this point suggested hyperactivity. As Jolene Raycox reread the report with Melissa sobbing in her mother's arms, the social worker in her yielded to the frustrated mother and felt she had misread the situation. Maybe at the worst, the mother had overreacted but not abusively, and not without cause. If so, all the mother would need is some counseling. Surely the doctors could find some other way to treat Melissa.

Ann Brown maintained her reserve and skepticism. She had to be shown otherwise. She was still unmoved and as team leader, her word would have more authority than Raycox's. The fact is she had been a social worker in child-abuse cases for some fifteen years. Jolene Raycox had been one for only two years. Ann Brown's credentials and work with the agency were exemplary. She had been a team leader for nearly seven years. She was now partnered with Raycox for nearly two years in order that Raycox would be trained properly with a veteran in the field. It was assumed that within several months, Ann Brown would be appointed case manager herself. She had the seniority, the experience, the recognition within the agency and she had applied for the position. When the agency wanted to explain what a social worker did and was, it pointed to Ann Brown. The agency fully expected some of Ann Brown would rub off on Jolene Raycox.

Jolene Raycox had received a high honor in being teamed up with Ann Brown. The agency felt when Raycox was hired that she had the potential of being one of their top social workers, but she had to be trained in the agency way by the best; thus, she was teamed with Ann Brown.

Ann Brown turned to Mrs. Gunnarsen and said, "Angela —may I call you Angela? I really need to talk to the children now, alone. Why don't I go upstairs with them and Jolene will stay here with you?"

One reason Ann Brown had maintained her reserve and skepticism and why she asked at this point to speak to the children alone was Nicole's response to her answering Melissa's question about removing the mother from the children. Nicole had been quiet — brutally quiet, not so much a whimper or a sigh — no sound from her whatsoever. Physically, she did not change facial color; she gave no involuntary body reactions. To a person with a trained eye as was Ann Brown's, the reaction of Nicole suggested the child expected or assumed the parent would be leaving under the circumstances. She took it in stride as if the possibility of removing a parent was but the natural consequence of what the parent had done.

Ann Brown wanted to explore that reaction privately and now, while the thought was still fresh in Nicole's mind. At this point, Mrs. Gunnarsen became highly resistant. There was no way she would allow the children to be interviewed privately. She insisted on her right to be present at the questioning. Brown and Raycox tried to reason with her, pointing out the necessity of finding out the truth of the situation, and that if the truth was that she did only what she said she did, she had nothing to be afraid of. Mrs. Gunnarsen, however, continued to resist, insisting that the social workers could and would manipulate the children into saying whatever the social workers wanted them to say.

Brown and Raycox denied this as even being possible. They cited studies showing that children do not lie about such matters. Further, the presence of the mother might intimidate the children. Only a private interview could secure the truth. Mrs. Gunnarsen would not hear of it.

Ann Brown calmly told Mrs. Gunnarsen that either she permit the interview or she would be forced to call the police. To emphasize the point and prove she was serious, Ann Brown walked to the phone. It was but a few yards away, visible to all the parties present and easily accessible to her. She picked up the phone, dialed the operator and stated, "This is a Children's Affairs Division emergency call. My code number is 630202. This is Ann Brown."

The operator checked into the computer, which could confirm or deny that such a call was genuine. The operator replied that the information was confirmed and she should state her emergency. Standard procedure is to ask the operator to hold and ask the client once more to give permission. If the client did so, the operator was told the emergency was hereby cancelled. If the client still refused, the operator was instructed to contact the local police and order they be sent out to the house to enforce the request of the division. Ann Brown put the operator on hold and following procedure, asked Mrs. Gunnarsen if it were necessary to call in the police. Mrs. Gunnarsen replied it was not — the social worker could talk to the children. Ann Brown cancelled the emergency.

While Jolene Raycox stayed with Mrs. Gunnarsen, Ann Brown escorted the children upstairs. Mrs. Gunnarsen was visibly agitated at this, and as a result, Jolene Raycox started asking Mrs. Gunnarsen all sorts of questions. Each in its own way would help the investigation along. Questions were asked about Mr. Gunnarsen, when he might return, his work, his relationship to the family, and specifically the children, who handled the discipline, who did the cooking, who did the cleaning, Mrs. Gunnarsen's out-of-the-house activities, where the family went on vacation last year, how often the children were out of school and for what reasons, who the family doctor was and how long they had lived in this house, among other questions.

In reply to these questions, it was discovered that the Gunnarsens had been in the state only six months. Mr. Gunnarsen's business had transferred him here. The family was still finding its way around. The children had been disoriented by the move as had Mrs. Gunnarsen. Raycox noted afterwards how the stress of the move could have impacted Mrs. Gunnarsen and made her abusive. Her husband's long hours could have complicated the situation, making her less likely to cope. She was the disciplinarian, he but rarely, as he was not home when discipline needed to be administered. She was the housewife extraordinaire, though tired of housework and maybe too tired of it, to the point of anger directed at Melissa for not being a housewife's dream child.

The children's school schedule here was normal but would be correlated with the school's reports. Since the family had been in the area a short time, the name of the family doctor in the previous residence was obtained. He would be contacted to see if there was a pattern of abuse. No specific answer could be given as to when Mr. Gunnarsen himself might return. The other information obtained in this interview was routine and held to be unimportant.

Meanwhile upstairs, Ann Brown had taken Melissa and Nicole first into the two girls' rooms and then into the master bedroom. This was done to obtain a geography of the events. Knowing what took place in each room, which room belonged to which person and the positioning of the participants in the context of the geography made it possible to ascertain the truth of the situation if accusations did arise from the children.

The children were told that their mother had admitted hitting Melissa hard and their mother wanted them to cooperate by telling Ann the truth. This way "Mommy" could be helped, and Melissa and Nicole could be helped. "You do want to help Mommy, don't you, Melissa and Nicole?" was the final question before the interrogation began.

At first the children were reluctant to answer the questions, but as Ann — as she kept calling herself and having the children call her when they spoke to her — kept prodding and using approved psychological teachings to get around their resistance, the children became cooperative. They stated what had been given at the beginning of this narrative. In response she gave them each one of her business cards and told them to call her or the official toll free number any time if any more such incidents occurred. The children were assured such behavior by their mother was inappropriate and not good for children. She was there to help them and her mother. She would make sure their mother never did this again.

She talked with the children about how they could protect themselves in the future. They were told that if they were afraid such an incident would recur, they should scream as loud as they could, they should try to run away, run out of the house, go to a neighbor's, go to the police or call the police from somebody else's house. In case of absolute necessity, one should try to distract their mother while the other ran for help. No one, however, should take undue risks. If all else failed, as soon as possible tell a teacher at school or the principal or someone else who could be trusted to call the state for help.

At this point, Nicole broke down and started to cry, followed by Melissa. Ann, seeing their tears, was herself caught up in the emotion of the moment and took hold of Melissa and cuddled the child in her arms. It was at this point that Mr. Gunnarsen walked into the room. He was told by a surprised Ann Brown that she was not through interviewing the children and would he be so kind as to wait downstairs. She then closed the door as he went down the stairs.

Mr. Gunnarsen had arrived home but a few moments previously. He had come home early from work to check up on his wife and children and found social worker Jolene Raycox talking with Mrs. Gunnarsen. He asked what was going on and was informed by Raycox that an official investigation was underway to determine if an abusive situation had occurred. Raycox was interviewing Mrs. Gunnarsen and her partner Ann Brown was interviewing the children upstairs. Since he was there now, she would like to ask him some questions. Mr. Gunnarsen asked how long the children had been upstairs. Mrs. Gunnarsen looked at her watch and estimated about an hour. Mr. Gunnarsen felt that was unacceptable and declared his intention to check on the children and see what was going on. Raycox tried to stop him but he ran up the stairs and hearing the speaking went in and saw the scene previously described. He headed back downstairs and went to his wife.

He took his wife aside for a few moments at which Jolene Raycox was not present. She felt they should have a few moments to themselves since this was the first he had known the investigation was going on. After approximately five minutes, she called out, "Mr. and Mrs. Gunnarsen, we do need to talk further."

The Gunnarsens returned. Mr. Gunnarsen sat to the left of Jolene Raycox, Mrs. Gunnarsen to the right. Mr. Gunnarsen was exceedingly hostile to the presence of Jolene Raycox and at this point was totally uncooperative.

Other than providing basic information about his work, he refused to answer any of Raycox's questions, no matter how she asked them. He kept interrupting with questions of his own, particularly with how long the children would be upstairs with the other social worker. Raycox could only reply as long as was necessary, but that it should not be much longer. Mr. Gunnarsen became more agitated as Raycox repeated this answer several times. By the third time she had given this answer, he jumped out of his chair and said loudly he would bring the children down if they did not come down immediately.

Upstairs, Ann Brown, after having been made aware of Mr. Gunnarsen's presence, was bringing her interview and consolation to a close. Mr. Gunnarsen's voice was loud enough to be heard throughout the house, and Ann Brown felt she had to go downstairs and into the living room as Mr. Gunnarsen was declaring that if they did not come down immediately, he would go up and get them.

Seeing the children, Mr. Gunnarsen immediately calmed down and embraced the girls. Both Melissa and Nicole were happy to see their father and almost seemed to jump into his arms. Both declared their love for their father and he reciprocated.

Seizing the moment, Ann Brown proceeded to question Mr. Gunnarsen about his whereabouts and his knowledge of the incident. He answered tersely but precisely as previously indicated. He volunteered no information. His answers were specifically formulated for the question he was asked. When Ann Brown and Jolene Raycox teamed up to try to prod him into providing more information, he became silent and simply shook his shoulders. When asked what that meant, he said, "Nothing."

Ann Brown bluntly asked if he were going to be more helpful, meaning more forthcoming, and he replied, "No."

Brown explained to him as previously to his wife the legal consequences of uncooperativeness, including calling in the police. He went to the phone and said, "Do you know the number? I'll call them myself and while I'm at it, I will call an attorney, if you don't mind."

Ann Brown declared neither was necessary at this point. This was an investigation; nobody was accusing anybody of anything. Besides, things could be handled, Mrs. Gunnarsen was open for counseling and Melissa was not hurt excessively. Furthermore, she had enough information now and wanted to thank them for their time.

The children had observed this whole scene but were quiet. They stayed around their father and appeared to avoid their mother. Melissa went so far as to sit on her father's lap toward the end of this scene until Ann Brown proclaimed the intention of leaving.

Our information on the Gunnarsen's actions and reactions after the departure of Brown and Raycox is sketchy. We do know the parents questioned the children about what they said upstairs to Ann Brown. We also know the parents talked to each other about the presence of the social workers. We do know that Mrs. Gunnarsen came to believe the children were manipulated by Ann Brown, as will become clear below.

Ann Brown and Jolene Raycox returned to their office and presented their report to the case manager. When each one was asked by the case manger what their recommendations were for this case, each one clearly declared that she was convinced the situation was dangerous enough to warrant either immediate removal of the children from the house or the removal of the mother, the second option being only if the case manager could be convinced that Mr. Gunnarsen was not an abuser too. Brown and Raycox did not like his attitude, but they felt he had not been abusive. Nevertheless, they wanted an outside opinion. In either scenario, this meant the presence of the case manager.

Regulations require that no children could be removed nor could a parent be removed from a situation without the additional approval of the case manager. Such person would be required to visit the family and make an independent assessment, confirming what the social workers' preliminary assessment had found and recommended. Regulations further require that when a case manager must make this determination, that person is to be accompanied by the police, who would (a) actually remove the children present under the direction of the case manager, and (b) ensure the protection of both the division workers and the children.

The case manager would go with the social workers and the police to the house of the children and proceed to question the parents and children appropriately. After deliberation and consultation, if necessary, with her superior, the office manager, the children of a parent could be involuntarily removed from the situation.

It is standard procedure when the situation progresses to this point that the complete team (police and division staff) converge on the residence in the evening when the family is all home. The police would be contacted prior to the convergence and directed to observe the home and ensure that all the family was present prior to the team's entry. Case manager Sharon Steinwitz accordingly called the local police and provided the prerequisite information and directions, citing the state law governing the procedures. The police did not know the case manager or these particular staff persons and thus insisted on credentials.

Steinwitz asked if they had a fax machine. They did and after making the appropriate connections, a copy of their credentials came through in seconds. The credentials were recognized as proper by the police and the procedures were instituted. Police records indicate arrival at seven-fifteen p.m. Originally, the team had planned to move in at seven-thirty p.m. but police surveillance indicated that Mr. Gunnarsen might be about to leave the house. If that happened prior to the team's entry, the team would at the least have to postpone entry until his return. At the worst, it would mean waiting another day to enter, but that could leave the children in serious jeopardy. Intervention without all family members present is difficult and produces complications the team would prefer to avoid. Among these would be legal ramifications such as insufficient legal notice prior to removing a child (courts have been known to chastise agencies for being impatient in such situations, to the point of rejecting the agency probe altogether in consequence).

Apart from the legal problems are the psychological problems. The agency appears too intrusive and bureaucratically insensitive when it intervenes without all parties present. A parent finding the children gone without having had the opportunity to say goodbye on being notified this would happen in many cases makes the agency's goal of reconciliation difficult.

On the other side, by going in at seven-fifteen p.m. instead of the planned seven-thirty p.m., the division staff were only able to endow the police perfunctorily with the knowledge needed to handle the case properly. The staff had a full-scale checklist and analysis to present to the police prior to entry. But such information needed all the time up to seven-thirty p.m., and even fifteen minutes less meant details had to be omitted. Such omission would create problematic situations. Indeed, this is why the situation developed as indicated below.

Ann Brown officially knocked at the door, as she was the senior social worker and one of the two the family would recognize. Mr. Gunnarsen answered the door. Seeing the police present, he became furious and was about to refuse entry when one of the police officers (there were two) informed Mr. Gunnarsen that under state law in a suspected child-abuse situation if the parent did not allow entry, the parents were to be arrested on the spot and the children seized and removed from the home. If the parents had not abused a child, there were no grounds for fear. Mr. Gunnarsen reluctantly relented and allowed the team entry; however. his mood was bitter.

He informed the team that he was considering obtaining a lawyer. Ann Brown said that was his right but that cooperation rather than legal confrontation in the present situation would be easier for all concerned. He did not call a lawyer. Ann Brown quickly introduced the case manager Sharon Steinwitz. Steinwitz explained it was necessary for her to interview the children and the parents in order to form her own opinion. The police were present because it might be necessary to take legal action, but she hoped that would be unnecessary and that all could work together. After all, the children were important, and as parents they surely could see the need for concern for their own children.

She explained she would like to interview the children with Ann Brown present to consider what happened. Mrs. Gunnarsen became hysterical at this point and shouted obscenities at Brown. She declared that her daughters had told her that Brown coerced them into saying there was abuse when in fact there was not. Mrs. Gunnarsen made a move in the direction of Brown, but Mr. Gunnarsen stopped his wife. Police officer Tom Gisowski also moved over to Mrs. Gunnarsen and informed the Gunnarsens that a repeat of such an outburst would mean immediate incarceration and the removal of the children.

Nicole and Melissa had been upstairs playing until they heard their mother scream. They both rushed downstairs and saw Mr. Gunnarsen's intervention and heard police officer Gisowski's comments. Nicole blanched. Melissa panicked and went into a frenzy. She ran throughout the house screaming, hitting at the wall, kicking furniture, even falling down and spinning around on the floor. She proclaimed she would not go, nobody would hurt her mother, she loved her parents, everybody was out to get her, meaning herself, Melissa. On her second pass to the foyer where the team stood, she suddenly veered at Ann Brown and kicked Brown in the left leg and started to punch her. Brown and Mr. Gunnarsen were prepared to stop this and would have, but the second police officer, Emilio Antonez, perceiving this as a threat to Brown, pounced on the child and knocked her to the floor.

This action, of course, was against regulations. A child would have had to display a weapon and been capable of using it before such action would be warranted. Neither situation was present here, and thus the officer's action was unacceptable. Naturally, the unfortunate deviance from regulations occurred because of the missing fifteen minutes. It was simply not possible to say all that had to be said before entry. Consequently, the police officer did not understand such behavior was improper. In light of the possibility that Mr. Gunnarsen would have left before the planned entry, any court would realize the inadvertence of the error and the importance of upholding the agency despite the incident.

Jolene Raycox was the first to regain composure and chastised the policeman publicly. She apologized to the family and to the children with a special apology to Melissa. She tried to explain that she knew Melissa was overwrought, that she knew Melissa was sometimes sick, that she understood the disease called hyperactivity and how it set her off at times of stress. She knew that Melissa was scared for her mother and herself, and it was okay to be afraid. Also she knew that being afraid like this could cause Melissa to go into hyperactive behavior and she understood that. So of course Melissa would try to strike out at her perceived enemies, especially Ann Brown. Ann had talked to her and was the one Melissa knew best and indeed would be the one to blame.

Jolene Raycox said if she were in Melissa's situation she would want to do what Melissa did. But she wanted Melissa to know that Ann, the police officer, Sharon, or herself, Jolene, were not her enemies but her friends there to help her if she would just let them. They wanted to help her parents too and not hurt anyone. They had to be sure she was safe and protected. Could she understand that?

Melissa indicated she could and calmed down. She immediately ran to her mother, who took Melissa in her arms and led her to a sofa in the nearby living room, where they both sat down. Mr. Gunnarsen asked the team to come into the living room. All did except Officer Antonez, who felt he had to stay by the door, just in case. Officer Gisowski moved to the left of Mrs. Gunnarsen and Melissa but remained standing yet keeping a watchful eye on the two. The other team members and Mr. Gunnarsen sat in various chairs around the living room.

Steinwitz again explained the necessity of her interviewing the children with Ann Brown present and not the parents. Mr. Gunnarsen said that would not be possible. He had been led to believe that Ann Brown manipulated the previous interview; consequently, he would not allow final action with regard to the children to occur without his presence and knowledge. Steinwitz relented and indicated he could go upstairs and listen to her interview the children provided, with Ann Brown being present as well. Mr. Gunnarsen was reluctant but agreed. The police would remain downstairs just in case, along with Raycox and Mrs. Gunnarsen.

Upstairs went the threesome plus the children. Brown remained in the background for the interview and never asked a question of the children. Both Steinwitz and Mr. Gunnarsen asked questions of the children. The interview reconfirmed the story already given. The children further indicated that their father had never beaten them, a light spanking once in a great while, but nothing serious.

On the other hand, Mrs. Gunnarsen had committed abuse previously to both children. Mr. Gunnarsen was visibly shocked and disturbed by the answer of the children. Though he pressed like a defense attorney to a hostile witness on the courtroom stand, the father could not shake the children from their story. Eventually, he broke into tears and had to be consoled by Steinwitz. When he broke into tears, Ann Brown also broke into tears.

Steinwitz was reminded by Brown's tears of Mrs. Gunnarsen's accusation and Mr. Gunnarsen's belief. She asked the children if they had been coerced, forced, in any way threatened by Ann Brown to tell this story. The children said no. They were further asked if because of anything Ann Brown said or did, the story were untrue. The children reaffirmed the validity of the story.

The children were asked to stay upstairs while Steinwitz would talk to the parents. When the threesome came downstairs, Mrs. Gunnarsen was seen to be visibly upset. Steinwitz pulled aside Raycox while Mr. Gunnarsen sat beside his wife and held her. Raycox indicated that Mrs. Gunnarsen was angry, hostile, nasty and mean during the time the threesome were upstairs. Her language was filthy, her tone harsh and no ordinary conversation could be carried on. Both police officers had become concerned and tried to quiet down Mrs. Gunnarsen but to no avail. Officer Gisowski felt the situation was getting out of control and he was about to place Mrs. Gunnarsen under arrest when the three came downstairs. Mr. Gunnarsen was now able to bring control back to his wife, which made the situation controllable again.

Steinwitz asked to speak to the parents with the social workers present. Mrs. Gunnarsen screamed that she would not talk to anybody as long as that _____ (obscenity deleted from official records) was present, meaning Ann Brown. Brown excused herself and said this was a time for Steinwitz to be alone with the parents. Officer Gisowski declared that he would not leave Steinwitz by herself with the Gunnarsens. Steinwitz replied that Gisowski could be close, just in case, but she needed privacy to deal with the situation. Gisowski complied.

23

Steinwitz and the Gunnarsens went into the kitchen, where seated at the kitchen table, Steinwitz repeated the basic outline of the children's story and asked for Mrs. Gunnarsen's comments. Mrs. Gunnarsen stuck by her previous story. Mr. Gunnarsen then repeated what he had heard and observed. Mrs. Gunnarsen screamed, "It's all a lie concocted by that _____ (same obscenity as previously, officially deleted) Ann Brown."

According to Mrs. Gunnarsen, Ann Brown manipulated the children. Mr. Gunnarsen pointed out that the children denied this. Steinwitz indicates she was impressed with Mr. Gunnarsen for doing this in front of her. It clearly convinced her he was not abusive and that he was upset with his wife for her actions. He did not go out of his way to protect his wife or keep her in a lie. He was willing to protect his children. This factor became an important point regarding the children as will become evident soon.

Mrs. Gunnarsen cried. Steinwitz said she was convinced that the children had told the truth and that she would be required to take some action on the children's behalf, perhaps moving them. Both Gunnarsens immediately reacted negatively to this news. Steinwitz said the alternative would be the removal of Mrs. Gunnarsen from the household. Mrs. Gunnarsen would have none of this. Mr. Gunnarsen was quiet, apparently reflecting on this. He asked what that meant. His wife became linguistically abusive to him. But he repeated the question.

Steinwitz said he would be responsible for the children. Mrs. Gunnarsen would have to see an approved counselor, preferably one arranged by the Children's Affairs Division. In any such situation, the counselor would have to provide regular detailed information about Mrs. Gunnarsen in order for the division to be able to ascertain when Mrs. Gunnarsen might be allowed to return. The division, after all, was not interested in destroying broken families but rather fixing them like a mechanic does the family car. The division was the mechanic in this case. Mrs. Gunnarsen would also have to leave the house that night or else the children could not stay. This meant arranging a place to stay for her. Were there friends or relatives who could be contacted that night and take her in for a time? Mr. Gunnarsen thought there were, but he would have to phone them first.

Mrs. Gunnarsen could not believe her ears and insisted either she or her children would have to be carried out, kicking and screaming all the way. Steinwitz insisted that while such could be arranged, it was not helpful and would definitely complicate any arrangements. Under the circumstances, it might be better to move the children than force Mrs. Gunnarsen into such behavior. Mr. Gunnarsen interrupted and asked to be allowed to speak to his wife alone. Steinwitz felt this was a good idea, said so and left the kitchen.

While we are not privy to that conversation, we do know the consequences. Mrs. Gunnarsen agreed to leave the house that evening. Mr. Gunnarsen would have control over the children. Mrs. Gunnarsen would see a division-authorized counselor, who would report regularly to the division on Mrs. Gunnarsen's progress. Mrs. Gunnarsen and Mr. Gunnarsen would sign papers, not legally binding, but rather acknowledging that the aforementioned agreement would indeed be the procedure in the present situation. Mrs. Gunnarsen was calm and composed. Thus, Steinwitz dismissed the police, feeling any threat in the situation was resolved. The police did tell Steinwitz that if she needed them, call and they would be right back. She did not call them back. Mr. Gunnarsen called a friend and though did not explain the situation on the phone, was able to arrange for housing for his wife. He did promise his wife would explain all upon arrival.

Mrs. Gunnarsen did pack up and leave. She was told prior to departure that if she forgot anything to call her husband and he would arrange for their pick-ups. Also, she was not to see the children for at least a week, possibly longer. The division would decide when that was best. Therefore, if she needed to come home for anything, she must do it before the children were released from school. The school would be notified of this provision as would the police. Nonetheless, all records would be confidential.

After Mrs. Gunnarsen's exit, Steinwitz instructed Brown and Raycox to return first to the office to clear up the paperwork and then go to their own homes for the night. Steinwitz and Mr. Gunnarsen were alone together. She said that how he acted in the interim would determine what happened to the children hereafter and when Mrs. Gunnarsen would return. The division would be of assistance in providing childcare and whatever other support might be needed. The division represented in Jolene Raycox would be contacting him daily at first to see how things were going and to offer any sort of help as might be needed. Mr. Gunnarsen was appreciative and said childcare would be his first need and he could use the services of the division to make that possible. Steinwitz assured him that would be Raycox's first priority. Steinwitz then left.

All indications are that the children slept well that night. Mr. Gunnarsen did not tell the children the full story until the next morning. Mrs. Gunnarsen was at a friend's house and the next day would come over to her house for more clothes but as agreed not at a time when the children were home.

Chapter 2

The Therapist's Notes

The following are various notes of Dr. Joan Prolewski, Ph.D. in psychology and M.D. in psychiatry, staff consultant to Children's Affairs Division (hereafter, for the sake of brevity using its abbreviation CAD), in light of her role as assigned therapist for Mrs. Angela Gunnarsen (nee Bonicelli).

(1)Initial Notes:

Mrs. Gunnarsen, hereafter designated Angela as per patient-doctor protocol, was in a very emotional state at the first session. She continually asked when she would see her children again. I had to inform her that such a question was premature and would depend upon how she responded to these sessions. It took most of the one-hour first session simply trying to calm her down. She could not focus on anything and could not respond to the most basic of questions. She was adamant that this was all a mistake and that she was "not some violent child abuser the agency was making me out to be," to use her words specifically.

Confronted with the facts, she did not deny them, but insisted this was a one-time event. She had never done anything like this before. For the record, it should be noted that CAD, after a thorough investigation of where the family had lived before, found no indication Angela had done anything like this before.

Hospital records, medical records, school records, neighborhood investigations, among others, all came back negative. Indeed, the universal response was that if such an event happened, it was atypical of Angela and must have been brought on by unusual circumstances.

Research did indicate that daughter Melissa had been under psychiatric regimen for confirmed hyperactivity, but that the regimen had been unsuccessful. Further, the family had invested substantial resources in various psychotherapies, all without success. Every report confirmed that Melissa was an extremely difficult child, and that her hyperactivity was severe. Some reports expressed amazement that Angela had not broken before, in light of Melissa's ongoing problems. The universal expert opinion was that, if anything, Mrs. Gunnarsen needed relief or assistance with Melissa. Mr. Gunnarsen's schedule made it difficult for him to be the relief or assistance his wife needed.

CAD was not pleased with the results of the research. It reflected badly on the agency, suggesting that the agency had overreacted. Perhaps if help had been provided, some proper relief for Angela, time away from Melissa, she would not have to be away from her daughters at all. However, now that the agency has separated Angela from the children, the process must be completed, as stated in the guidelines. My involvement meant helping Angela Gunnarsen deal with her anger, her potential for abuse, and finding alternative ways for her to relate to her children, especially Melissa with her attendant issues.

Interestingly, in light of the official report made available to me before the session, Angela's language to me was civil and correct. There was no hint even at the most emotional of obscenity. The anger, however, was real. She was angry at CAD. She was angry at her husband for allowing her to be separated from her children. She was angry that she was reported in the first place instead of counseled. She was angry that she was here, feeling this was totally unnecessary. And she clearly and most emphatically was angry with me.

Because of her anger as well as the separation, I had to ignore the research and assume she was a child abuser. The facts said differently, but the separation had happened. Even accepting that the agency had overreacted, I was required to ignore anything but the separation and deal with that reality. The separation had happened; therefore, she was a child abuser — period. I was not given latitude in the situation, or allowed to dismiss or disregard the situation. The only way the agency would allow the mother to reunite with the children once a separation had been formulated was to inculcate a program of alternative behaviors in Mrs. Gunnarsen. That was my sole responsibility. Consequently, this is how I related to Mrs. Gunnarsen.

I would discover in the process that she hoped for an advocate or at the least someone who could understand her position, but I could not be that person.

(2)Notes from Session 3:

As indicated previously, Angela Gunnarsen was both emotional and hostile to the process, but because she had no choice, realizing this was the only way she would be reunited with her children, she has gradually relented and participated. Rewards for particular behaviors are approved psychological technique and do produce significant behavioral changes. Angela simply confirmed this.

CAD has officially inquired whether I saw it as appropriate to medicate Angela, perhaps with tranquilizers or mood-altering pharmacologies. I have reserved that option, which only I can prescribe as per my medical degree. Nonetheless, I am required to respond officially to such an inquiry by CAD. My official response was that such an action was premature. I have not met with her long enough to decide whether medication or counseling, or a combination of both techniques, would be the most advantageous for Angela.

As indicated above, Angela is now participating in the process. To my surprise, she talked about Melissa's hyperactivity and how that has impacted her reactions to

Melissa. Pharmacological treatments may provide the only possible amelioration of Melissa's situation, though as indicated earlier, that is no excuse or rationalization for child abuse. These notes are subject to review by CAD and thus, as per guidelines, must reflect that child abuse can not be excused under any circumstances.

It may be necessary to provide a contracted program for regular separations of mother and child, so that mother is not tempted to give in to child abuse when circumstances are difficult. Nonetheless, I have also informed Angela that child abuse is child abuse under any and all circumstances and must be addressed. Her face tightened, her hands contracted to fists, and her eyes glared, but she said nothing. At that point, I ended the session.

(3)Notes from Session 6:

It should be noted that as per Angela Gunnarsen's request, we have been meeting daily. She realizes that once progress is made she can be reunited with her children, if at least temporarily for visitation purposes. We have talked about her anger and ways she can control it. This, of course, is teaching her anger management. I have provided a pamphlet of approved techniques and had her practice some as the session wound down. These include controlled breathing, a personal time-out for Angela instead of her daughter, the old counting to ten before saying or doing anything to Melissa, forcing herself to focus on other activities she is engaged in so that Melissa's actions will not ruin her disposition or distract her, making a point to praise Melissa for the good she does, especially when Melissa does badly so that anger at Melissa does not boil over. If these do not work, sit down, leave the room, call out to her husband or even her other daughter if available to explain to Melissa what she has done. I will introduce her to biofeedback as well in a subsequent session. And I have told her that if she feels ultimately unable to stop the anger, I will prescribe medications, which she is to take when the anger surges. These are but a sample of the techniques available and listed in the approved pamphlet, but they are cited in order that review may note they were suggested and demonstrated.

Finally, it must be stated for the record that I gave her my own personal cell phone number. Thus, she can reach me twenty-four hours a day. If all else fails, talking to me on phone will stop her from reacting inappropriately. Alcoholics Anonymous created this technique to "save" alcoholics from falling back into alcohol. It has proven to be remarkably successful and as a result has been picked up by the whole therapy community as an essential ingredient in any therapeutic situation.

(4)Notes from Session 7:

It has been pointed out to me that I have not been providing enough information about Angela's comments, feelings or what is actually going on inside Angela. It has been stated that my notes previously treated her as an object instead of a subject. My notes are also subject to peer review, meaning other professionals in the field. They have informed me that I must let the person of Angela Gunnarsen emerge in my notes, or the notes will be incomplete and inadequate. Indeed, Angela Gunnarsen cannot be understood unless she is speaking for herself. In response to these comments, I will submit selected verbatims of our sessions together. A verbatim is simply the written account of our conversations in our sessions. They are as accurate as a court stenographer's recording of a legal deposition, which then becomes a legal transcript for all subsequent hearings. The only difference between a legal transcript and a verbatim is that per psychological procedures, a verbatim may include editorial additions about physical presence, emotions displayed, body motions, involuntary actions, etc. These additions are enclosed in parentheses.

Because this is a matter of child abuse, the state waives doctor-patient confidentiality issues. Angela Gunnarsen was informed of this waiver at her first meeting with me. Everything she says to me must at my discretion and CAD's request be available for scrutiny. The point is that progress can then be visibly demonstrated by Angela and she may then be reunited with her children. Thus, while she is talking to me one on one, she is through me talking to a wide variety of professionals working on her case.

The following is an appropriate verbatim of portions of Session 7, using our first names to designate the speaker:

ANGELA: When will I get to see my children again?

JOAN: We believe it will be soon. However, it will be short and supervised.

ANGELA: You don't trust me?

JOAN: It is not a matter of trust, it is rather a first step toward full reintegration with your children. And as a first step, like in walking, you must take baby steps and be watched over before you can walk fully on your own.

ANGELA: You can call it what you will, but you still don't trust me.

JOAN: There are procedures we must follow. This first step is state-mandated and can not be circumvented regardless of how you feel about it. The real question is whether you are willing to accept this procedure or not.

ANGELA: Do I really have any choice?

JOAN: No. (Angela looks chagrined, she bites her lip. Therefore, I respond.) How does that make you feel?

ANGELA: Not exactly overjoyed. But when it is put that way, I may fret about it, but I will live with it. (Her voice suggests resignation.)

JOAN: There are many things in life we have to live with though we are not exactly overjoyed about them.

ANGELA: No doubt.

JOAN: Melissa, for example.

ANGELA: Yes, I know, I let my frustrations get to me and I overreacted.

JOAN: The fact you can say that is definitely positive. Self-realization of inappropriate behaviors is a clear beginning in self-awareness of the necessity of change.

ANGELA (laughing): Doctor, you are too much into psychological jargon. You can't say it simply that knowing what

I did was wrong will force me to think before ever doing that again.

JOAN: We all have our own ways of communicating. If I use "jargon," as you say, it is because that is my training and that is who I am. If you do not use "jargon," as you say, it is because that is not part of your training and, therefore, not who you are. We are all different, as is Melissa.

ANGELA: You keep coming back to Melissa.

JOAN: Melissa is why we are here at all.

ANGELA (appearing wistful): Yes, that is why we are here at all. I wish to God it had never happened.

JOAN: That too is definitely positive. I won't respond to this psychologically, but let's just say that suggests you are, to use your language, aware of what was wrong and that you should not do it again. The wrong actions do produce unfortunate consequences.

ANGELA (laughing again): I'm sorry, it just seems you have a line for everything I say.

JOAN (I sigh here): Yes, I know. I guess it just comes with the territory. But you are still not speaking about Melissa *per se*.

ANGELA: I know, I know. Melissa is my problem child, my hyperactive child, who knows how to get to me. She rings my bell hard, and I respond (she pauses) inappropriately. I do have to work on controlling my temper, my impatience, my (she pauses again as if in thought, but seeing her face one can tell she cannot find another word and, therefore, simply says) my whatever.

JOAN: It is the whatever we have to discover and dissect or at least control. And this is probably as good a place as any to stop for this session. I will see you tomorrow at the same time.

(5)Notes from Session 10:

In this session, Angela defines what she called the "whatever." For evaluation purposes, I have chosen to attach the following verbatim:

JOAN: Tell me about your parents.

ANGELA (clearly caught off guard by this question): Huh?

JOAN: Sometimes what we experienced as a child of parents has an impact on how we parent. So tell me about your parents.

ANGELA (defensively): I loved my parents! They were the best parents in the world to me!

JOAN: I can accept that. But tell me what they were like as parents.

ANGELA: They loved me! They cared for me! They were my parents. (She is still defensive and this line of questioning is getting nowhere. Hence, I will have to try a different approach.)

JOAN: And your parents let you get anything you wanted or do anything you wanted?

ANGELA: I didn't say that.

JOAN: What are you saying then?

ANGELA: They loved me, they cared for me, but of course they put limits on me as any good, loving, caring parent would do.

JOAN: No doubt, as I or any parent would do. Where did they put limits on you?

ANGELA: Well, I couldn't talk unless spoken to. I always had to be one step behind my father and mother whenever we went anywhere. I didn't do anything without their permission.

JOAN: You know when I was a kid, there were times I didn't do what my parents wanted me to do and I got in trouble.

ANGELA: Well, sure I got in trouble at times.

JOAN: My parents put me in a corner or up in my room or took away some privileges.

ANGELA: My father belted me.

JOAN: With a belt?

ANGELA: Yeah (face fallen as if this is too painful to remember, but remember she must).

JOAN: That must have hurt.

ANGELA (looks at me with disdain as if I am stupid): That's the point.

JOAN (I don't back down): Even so, it must have hurt really bad.

34

ANGELA: Of course it did, but I knew it was for my own good.

JOAN: Is that what you said to yourself after it happened or did you have doubts if it really was for your own good?

ANGELA: Hey, I was a kid. How should I know…(her eyes light up but she stops speaking and tightens her lips together as if she felt she had said too much. I cannot let this get away).

JOAN: You were a kid, so how should you know that it was not really for your own good, that in fact what he did to you was wrong?

ANGELA: My father was a good man.

JOAN: I have no doubt about that, but he still hit you inappropriately. He still overreacted as you have overreacted. Sometimes what we have experienced incorrectly as a child can have bad influences on us as adults. If a parent hits us improperly as a child, we in turn hit back as an adult.

ANGELA: But as you know this was a one-time thing. I had never done anything like this before.

JOAN: That is quite true, but push comes to shove, in a difficult situation, instead of controlling yourself, you imitated your father. And as our agency believes, once that happens, it can happen again. Therefore, we have to prevent that from happening. Only as you can see that what your father did was wrong and how it has impacted you can we prevent it from surfacing again.

ANGELA: I told myself I was not going to be like my father in raising my children.

JOAN: And by all accounts you weren't, until Melissa…

ANGELA: Until Melissa pushed me just too far and I snapped, I instinctively acted like my father would in that situation (she is almost emotionless as she says these lines, she simply realizes the truth of them).

JOAN: Yes, you did, but that does not have to happen again if we can get you to think through and work on those techniques of self-control we have been dealing with.

ANGELA: I don't want to be like my father. I really don't want to be like my father (she cries at this point. I offer her a tissue. She takes it, wipes her eyes and continues). I am not going to be like my father. I won't. I can't. I will not let it happen. No, no, no.

JOAN: Because you realize this, you won't be. (It should be noted that some of my colleagues felt this statement was promising too much. What if she did repeat? What does that make of me? She would not be able to trust me again because I should have known better than to make assurances I personally cannot guarantee. I understand their point, and it is a valid one. Nonetheless, under the circumstances and in light of what I know about Angela Gunnarsen, I believe it to be true. I realize faith in someone or believing in someone is not accepted therapy in every psychological school, but I cannot operate that way. For me it is too cynical an approach to humanity. As a psychiatrist and psychologist, I have to offer hope otherwise why am I in this profession? I have to believe people can change and change dramatically or I may as well just walk away from what I am doing. I remain convinced this statement had to be made. I closed the session shortly after this.)

(6)Notes prior to Session 14:

CAD, at my request and after their own intra-office consultations and their own discussions with Mrs. Gunnarsen, allowed Angela to meet with her children. As indicated previously, this was a supervised meeting under CAD control. CAD has a strict policy that the first meeting lasts but thirty minutes. This is strictly timed and the mother is made aware of this policy before the first meeting. Typically, CAD has to physically separate mother and children at the finishing time. The children do not want to see their mother go, and the mother does not want to see the children go. CAD has to act in this situation like a cad (it should be noted that my humor on this topic is not appreciated by the agency. I have been so instructed to note that while the abbreviation of the agency is CAD, this does not in any form or fashion denote the agency's true nature, and attempts to say or write otherwise are inaccurate).

Anyway, following such a meeting, it is mandatory for the mother to debrief immediately (not more than one hour subsequent) with the therapist. Therefore, the first meeting is coordinated with my schedule, so that this debriefing may take place appropriately. It is expected that anger will be part of the mother's response and the therapist is called upon to anticipate and defuse this. More importantly, from the agency's perspective, the therapist must "get a feel" for how the mother responds to her children. This feeling determines the next meeting and how it is to be handled, or if there is even a next meeting.

Despite the agency's urgings, I have constantly refused to provide a verbatim to the agency on any of the first meeting debriefings. The emotions are too raw and the words do not reflect what the person is about. The agency believes in the power of the words and the emotions to guide them. This is simply not psychologically accurate, and I have given them appropriate readings from psychological field research to no avail. Therefore, I have simply refused to provide this verbatim, for which position I am constantly officially chastised (a lesser criticism than a reprimand, which would become part of my personnel record. Chastising is verbal, telling me my position is not in accord with their policies, and thus they do not accept my position but will not take any official action against me).

(7)Summation of Session 14:

Angela Gunnarsen was upset at the short duration of the visit. She pointed out repeatedly that the children screamed for their mother as she and they were separated. Melissa was the most adamant, and as the agency informed me and Mrs. Gunnarsen reiterated, Melissa became physically abusive toward the CAD representative. Melissa did attack that representative, and surprisingly for a small child, managed to force the CAD representative to the floor. On the floor, the child threw blows at the representative and repeatedly called the representative an evil woman. The action by Melissa was so swift and unexpected (despite all that has been reported by me and the agency's own investigation) that it took the agency by surprise and more than a few minutes to extricate the child from the representative.

Angela felt this proved the agency had overreacted, and this particular representative was clearly a problem. Since this representative, who will be unnamed herein, has a distinctive record and is highly regarded, the accusations appear baseless. These accusations arose from a hyperactive child, who does have serious psychological problems, and they cannot be taken seriously. Nonetheless, the attack has forced the agency to deal with Melissa, to which Mrs. Gunnarsen has been informed. Specifically, Melissa will be provided psychological help at the agency's expense. If the mother and child are to be reunited, obviously such actions by Melissa must be ameliorated.

Mrs. Gunnarsen's reactions to her children were under the circumstances appropriate and within proper psychological bounds. She clearly loves her children and wants only the best for them. As a mother, she naturally feels her presence is the best for her children. I assured her that the visits would continue for a time, but that eventually she would have unmonitored visits. Given enough time and patience as well as continued therapy, she would eventually receive her children back. She understands this, but she wonders how this may be affecting her children. And, she added, "What about my husband?"

I have not dealt with Mr. Gunnarsen in these sessions, and the agency is uncomfortable if not averse to allowing me to deal with him in these sessions. The agency has given him a clean bill of health, or as clean a bill of health as the agency gives anybody. CAD generally qualifies every evaluation, even the most positive. I do not fully understand that, and despite attempts to receive explanations, I have never received a satisfactory explanation. From another perspective altogether, it seems to me the agency takes seriously the theological concept of total depravity. Since the agency is secular, it does not specifically say this. However, the agency in its own writings clearly is convinced that no one is perfect and that everyone is flawed in certain ways. The agency is dealing with imperfect people doing improper behaviors, and every adult family member is more or less responsible and acting out their various flaws. Since the agency cannot take on the world, it must limit its and my investigation to the actual abuser. The agency and I are to restore broken relationships, but in such a manner that the imperfect can function in acceptable ways. Realizing their constant temptation to regress into abusive patterns, we are committed to providing them the tools needed for them to fight the temptations.

In specific response to Angela Gunnarsen's question about her husband, I can only assure her the agency will be helpful, but not intrusive, and will work with him in ways that he finds acceptable. Indeed, I know the agency has arranged for daycare for the children while he works. I know this is not what Mrs. Gunnarsen was asking, but it is the best response I can give in light of the preceding.

(8)Notes prior to Session 17:

The agency did provide a second opportunity for Angela to meet with her daughters. In light of what happened previously, however, the agency did provide a security person and an extra agency representative for the meeting. Both were fully informed as to Melissa's violence and were fully capable of stopping such, if it happened again. Fortunately, Melissa was under control this time, but she did make it a point never to look at the representative she attacked and called evil. Even when spoken to directly by that representative, she responded to the other representative. The victimized representative thereafter became silent and deferred totally to her colleague. The security person called the meeting totally uneventful, and did not so much as find any one occasion to put him on his guard. Melissa was that well-behaved.

As per mother-daughter interaction, I will leave that for the verbatim I will submit for session 17. Suffice it to say, neither I nor the agency feel regular visits are unwarranted. Therefore, after today the visits will become regular, to the point of daily, even if for only a few moments. If they go as planned, our constant work together will be reduced first to a weekly schedule, then a monthly schedule, at which time mother and daughters should be reunited under one roof with the husband/father.

It is also now my official opinion and declaration that Angela Gunnarsen does not need a pharmacological regimen. Therefore, that possibility is hereby removed from the work with Mrs. Gunnarsen. It is my professional opinion that she can improve and handle all situations appropriately in the future by talking to her therapist, and of course, her therapist providing her with the needed tools to be able to handle situations.

(9)Session 17 (verbatim):

JOAN: How did your second visit go with the girls?

ANGELA: Much better. They did ask me when I was coming home.

JOAN: How did you answer that question?

ANGELA: I told them, Mommy needs some help and as soon as she gets helped, she will come home. But it would be a while yet.

JOAN: A very good response, and what did they say?

ANGELA: They said, "We love you, Mommy, don't you love us?"

I said, "You know I do, my sweeties, and I promise all of us will be together again, but for now we have to be patient and wait until I am better again."

Melissa said, "Oh, then you are sick, like me?"

And I responded, "Yes, I am a bit sick, but a good doctor is helping to make me well." Melissa came over and hugged me. She said, "Mommy, I am so sick no one thinks I can get well."

JOAN (interrupting): Excuse me, but where did she get that idea?

ANGELA: That was precisely my immediate question. "The evil lady says so. The doctor I see now agreed with the evil lady when they thought I wasn't listening."

I took Melissa up in my arms and told her, "I don't care what anyone says. You are going to get well too. You'll see me get well and then you can know you will get well too." Melissa just buried herself on my breasts and cried. I held on to her, tears welling up in my eyes, and she picked up her head and looked at me while she said, "If you get well, Mommy, I promise I will get well too, no matter what anyone else says." I admit I got a lump in my throat, and I was afraid I was going to go into a full-scale cryfest. But somehow I managed to keep control. (At this point, Angela reached for the tissues and started to cry. I let her and did not intervene. It was only after she finished crying and regained composure that I spoke.)

JOAN: I can see that was hard on you, but you are doing much better, so that was an appropriate response. Tell me about other aspects of that visit, which were important to you.

ANGELA: Nicole hugged me too and told me she loved me. Sometimes, with all that has happened between Melissa and myself, I forget my lovely Nicole. She smiles at me, she puts her head in my side, and she pats me like I was her favorite cat. In turn, I smiled at her, I even laughed a little, and told her she was always special to me. Oh, she's a cutie. She always lights up my day, even when it is the darkest. And that situation she just made so much more bearable by being herself. Sweet Nicole!

JOAN: That's wonderful! I know we haven't said as much about Nicole in our conversations together, but then you have just explained why.

ANGELA (laughs): Yes, good, sweet Nicole! (sighs)

JOAN: What's the sigh for?

ANGELA: I imagine this has been the hardest on her. She keeps a lot of things inside and tries to manage a situation. She's our little peacekeeper, and the one who can't handle change too well. This is a changing situation, and she must really be on edge. I hope Andrew (her husband) is comforting her.

JOAN: I hear that he is doing well with both girls.

ANGELA: I'm glad to hear that. I hope I can be the mother they really need when I do go home. (Pauses) But I really don't know what to make of Melissa calling (name of CAD representative deleted at this point) evil. Why would she do that?

JOAN: Sometimes children project feelings onto somebody or something outside of a situation. Some children pick up a teddy bear or a favorite toy and start saying, "Bad teddy. Bad, bad." Of course, the teddy is not bad, but that is how they let out what is happening. She may be doing the same with (name deleted).

ANGELA: I hope so. Melissa doesn't say such about people, and I have never seen her attack someone outside the family before.

Personal comments: Further research has shown both the agency and me that Angela's statement at this point is quite correct. No one has ever heard Melissa call anyone evil, nor has she ever attacked anyone before. She may be getting more out of control with her mother gone, or maybe the projection has taken hold as a truth in the situation, despite how untruthful this may be. There is another possibility, something that would involve the CAD representative, but that seems highly unlikely in light of that person's high regard.

The rest of the session was spent talking about the interpersonal dynamics of the three of them. Specifically, I affirmed her love, her good gifts as a mother and how she was making progress. The way she dealt with her children in the latest visit was very positive and showed she was indeed moving in the right direction.

(10)Notes prior to Session 30:

I have not enclosed any more notes because from session 17 on, everything has been cut and dry. The patient, if that is what she is, Mrs. Angela Gunnarsen, has made remarkable progress. We have field tested some behavior techniques and biofeedback with Melissa present. Melissa was put into situations whereby her hyperactivity would manifest itself and it did. Using the techniques, Angela Gunnarsen was able to resist striking back, and in effect was able to turn the other cheek, but at the same time was able to control and discipline Melissa in appropriate ways.

Her talks with me have allowed her to face up to her past and her present. She is aware of her nature and what pushes her buttons, as it were. She is now able to restrain herself successfully in times of rising emotional anger. She calls me occasionally and I help her talk through her fears, her doubts, her self-control issues. Therefore, it is my professional opinion that after this session Angela Gunnarsen be discharged from regular therapeutic sessions with me and that barring any crisis, she will not see me again for six months. If after that six-month session everything is satisfactory, I will suggest another meeting one year thereafter. If that meeting is also concluded as expected, that will be our very last meeting together.

Elsewise, I hereby recommend to the agency that Mrs. Angela Gunnarsen (nee Bonicelli) be hereby discharged from the agency's caseload and that she be allowed full and free reunification with her children at her home.

(11) Session 30:

Something has happened that was not expected, involving the agency and not Mrs. Gunnarsen. Mrs. Gunnarsen, after moving back temporarily with the children prior to moving back permanently, was told disturbing news by the children dealing with the representative denoted as "evil" by Melissa.

BY ORDER OF DISTRICT JUSTICE M. EDWARD WINTHROP OF THE 15TH DISTRICT, THE FOLLOWING NOTES AND ALL SUBSEQUENT NOTES DEALING WITH THIS CASE ARE HEREBY CLOSED TO ALL BUT THIS COURT'S PERUSAL. IT IS FURTHER ORDERED THAT IN ALL PREVIOUS NOTES WHEREIN THE NAME OF THE REPRESENTATIVE OF THE CHILDREN'S AFFAIRS DIVISION WAS GIVEN THAT NAME IS TO BE DELETED.

Chapter 3

Andrew Gunnarsen's Take

He had a slightly disconcerting habit of referring to himself in the third-person singular instead of the first-person singular whenever his work required him to write down his take on a given situation. His bosses were never quite sure what to make of that habit. And they told him so. He assured them he would try to do better in the future, but he never could. Now as he was reflecting on how his own family life had been turned upside down, he could not say the first-person singular.

Yes, these are the reflections, the take, as it were of Andrew Gunnarsen, how he perceives the whole scenario. He really did not like the social workers when they were at the house and thereafter. He knew they had exaggerated a situation into a setting whereby they could justify their existence. Yes, his wife had hit Melissa. Yes, he knew she had done more than a hard slap. Yes, his wife had abused Melissa. Yes, yes, yes. He knew this was true, but they still went beyond the pale. It could have been handled so differently, so cooperatively, so compassionately.

But these were bureaucrats of the stereotypical Kafka fame, and compassion was not in their vocabulary. That Ann Brown was the worst. He has never seen such a cold, calculating, cruel woman. There is something about her that reeks of evil. He is being judgmental, biased, unfair — maybe the first two, but not the last. There is something about her that is wrong, and he does not know what.

Ann Brown dominated her colleague. She held on to Melissa as if she were her own possession, her own toy. What a word, a toy! He had a way with reflections, his bosses said his reflections were always accurate and insightful. He could see into situations that no one else could. His analysis always held up. His ability to read people was infallible. Something was wrong about Ann Brown, but he did not know what.

Fortunately, the next day he only had to deal with Jolene Raycox. She had a medical awareness even if she was a social worker. Thus, at the least she was understanding though not forgiving.

"Mr. Gunnarsen, can I call you Andrew or Andy?"

"No, you will call me Mr. Gunnarsen."

"Very well, Mr. Gunnarsen. With your work schedule, you may need some help watching the children, and…"

"What do you mean?" he interrupted quite loudly.

Jolene Raycox breathed out forcibly and audibly. "I mean the agency can help provide childcare, if needed. We do not want you to feel we are uncaring and have left you in a lurch."

He tried to control his temper, but he could not. "If the agency was so caring," he made sure the words came out sarcastically as well, "it would not have taken my wife out of my household." He surprised himself that he could use the first-person singular in conversations but not when he was writing. Maybe he could blame that affliction on some English teacher he had, but he could not think of one who pushed that piece of grammar on him.

"I realize you are angry and you have had to make decisions suddenly. No doubt, you have been put in a tough situation and all I am trying to say is that the agency and I are here to help you."

He calmed down a bit, but not entirely. "Well, until I can find a competent babysitter, I will need someone to watch the children during the day; that is, after school, until I get home.

For the time being, I will monitor my schedule so that I may be home by six p.m."

"I have a list of names here of people nearby who could fill that role."

"Why am I not surprised?" They seemed to have an answer for everything. "Very well, use my phone and arrange for someone, tomorrow perhaps, unless that is too soon."

"Let me see. I'll make the calls and get right back to you."

She was efficient that one. The first phone call worked out. Was he beginning to wonder if she had preplanned that response? Or was he just paranoid? She suggested he take the children over to meet the lady.

The babysitter's name was Wanda Branski. She was a little woman, but strong. She was past her childbearing years, but she loved children, so she was always willing to help the agency out. That is what she said anyway, and though he was inclined to dismiss such talk as gibberish, she sounded sincere. He gave her the benefit of the doubt, reluctantly. She told the kids to call her Granny Wanda.

Melissa, true to form, immediately asked, "Why? You're not my grandmother!"

Nicole turned to Melissa and said, "No, she is not, but she wants us to think of her like our grandmother, since grandmother is nice. And she wants to be nice like her."

"Why, Nicole, I think we are going to get along just fine," reciprocated Granny Wanda. He found himself even thinking of her with that designation. But how could he not? She had pure gray hair. Her skin was wrinkled and her face showed age. She was the type that let aging happen to her. He doubted if she had ever thought of going to a plastic surgeon. Anyway, she had to be up there in age.

"If you don't mind me asking," he found himself saying, "just how old are you, Granny Wanda?"

"I don't mind at all. I happen to be seventy-six and one month from today I will be seventy-seven."

"As to my schedule," he began.

"Jolene has already filled me in on the details. Never you mind, the little ones will be ready for your pickup. The school bus will drop them off here right after school; that has already been arranged by Jolene too."

He puckered his lips; he really did not want to speak. He knew he would say something particularly nasty. After all, wasn't he still the father? Didn't he have some say in all of this? But he held back and simply gurgled out, "Thank you." It was not one of his better efforts, but he could tell from Jolene and Granny Wanda that it would suffice.

On the ride back home, Jolene pointed out that under the circumstances the agency for a while would pay the babysitter. As soon as he was able to, he would be expected to make some contribution. That would all be negotiated, unless it became too difficult and then the agency would waive the costs altogether. But she was sure he would be able to contribute after he received his next paycheck in two weeks.

By this time, he was no longer surprised. She had done her homework on him thoroughly, even to finding out when he would receive paychecks. *It figures*, he thought. They are going to know everything public about himself. Thus, he must not allow her or anyone associated with the agency from knowing who he is, what he is as a person. Who knows how they would digest that, or whether they would use such information against him. He really could not let that happen, especially with the children needing him there, now that mother was not. They can make him a father, that is okay, but they will not control him, possess him, or in any way, shape or form, mold him. This is going to be difficult enough for the family; it will be worse if the agency dictates.

Thus, the next day while he was on the road for company business, he pulled into a gas station and called an attorney. In his work, he regularly heard comments about attorneys in the area, and there was one with a medium-sized firm whose name kept coming up: King McMasters. Besides, he was African-American as was Jolene Raycox and that meant the agency could not play games with King like they could with other attorneys. It would look like discrimination, even racism, if the agency came down on McMasters. And the word on the street was that King McMasters used his race brilliantly on behalf of his clients. But that did not mean King — he loved being called King by everybody, it put him in the driver's seat with everybody — would be his attorney. King McMasters chose his clients carefully and he refused more people than he accepted.

The white secretary of King McMasters took him to King. McMasters was with his white paralegal, who deferred to King shamelessly. And King ate it up — loved it. He explained the situation to the attorney and the attorney listened carefully, taking notes occasionally on his yellow legal pad.

"I have a retainer fee," King began.

"I believe this is your fee," he interrupted as he gave the attorney a prepared check.

"Precisely. Jim," he turned to his paralegal, "get the paperwork for our new client."

Jim ran out the door and was back in two minutes flat. He gave all the necessary paperwork to McMasters, who passed it over to Andrew Gunnarsen.

Gunnarsen chose not to read a word; no matter what the paperwork said, he would abide by. Whatever it took he would have King McMasters. King was impressed when Gunnarsen simply signed the paperwork. "I could explain it to you." King felt as a lawyer he ought to make that gesture.

"No. Here." He gave the paperwork back to McMasters, who handed it to Jim. And Jim quickly left the office, no doubt to process the paperwork.

"So CAD is living up to its name?" asked McMasters.

"Yes, yes, yes," he said as tears involuntarily welled up in his eyes.

"I *will* get you through it."

He believed King would.

Precisely at six p.m., after he had finished feeding the children, the phone rang. McMasters had informed him that before the day was out, the agency would be receiving a phone call informing them of the new legal status. McMasters warned him that the agency would no doubt call, one of the two social workers to be precise, with the explicit purpose of trying to convince him to drop legal representation.

"No matter what the individual may say, refuse and refer her to my office." McMasters repeated this line and then forced Andrew to use the words.

"They are very intimidating."

"I know, that's how they get away with what they do. That's their job. This is my job, and I can be as intimidating as they can be. I will handle them, not you. From this point on, anything concerning the kids, your wife, the situation, will be cleared through me. I will do what you can't. That is what you are paying me for, and I do my job."

McMasters spoke with an authority and conviction that I could not deny. He was impressed; he actually used the first-person singular. But he saw he went right back to the third-person singular. He knew it could not last. It has to be some sort of self-defense mechanism.

"Good evening."

"Mr. Gunnarsen, this is Ann Brown."

"Yes." He thought about saying more, but he was not going to be helpful, responsive or even civil to them.

"How are you doing this evening?" she was trying to be civil, even if he was not.

"Fine," is all he replied.

"Good. I am glad to hear it." She paused, obviously expecting him to respond and say more. He didn't and the phone was silent. She finally broke the silence with, "The agency has been notified you have hired legal counsel, a Mr. King McMasters. Is that correct?"

"Yes, it is."

She again waited for him to say more, but he didn't. "The agency really does not feel that is necessary. We have been handling the matter so well, and you have been exemplary. A lawyer will just slow the process down, and I know you don't want that."

One of the warnings McMasters had given him was that they would indirectly threaten to slow the process down. They would no doubt blame McMasters for any slowdown. The legal process, they would say, clearly has built into it roadblocks that guarantee matters will take longer to resolve than without a lawyer. "Don't believe that garbage."

Jim involuntarily whistled. McMasters smiled at his paralegal, and said to him, "Oh, you thought I was going to use my favorite four-letter word that begins with an s, huh?"

Jim smiled nervously, but did not respond. McMasters replied, "Relax, Jim, you know me too well. I am trying to be on my best behavior, even if you know what I think of that agency."

Jim found his voice, "You don't think much of *that* agency!"

"No, I don't. And that is the biggest reason I am taking your case, Mr. Gunnarsen. If I can screw those," he paused. Jim was looking right at him, expecting King to say another obscenity. King smiled, "those so-and-sos, I will. They need to be put in their place and realize they are human beings dealing with human beings once and for all. The legal system is the only defense you have against them, and you cannot let them take that away from you. If you do, you and your family are screwed."

"Mr. McMasters is my attorney and will remain so. If you have anything to say to me, you will say it to him. From now on, all communications from the agency regarding my family and this situation will go through him."

"Mr. Gunnarsen, I am just trying to say that without a lawyer this process will go so much quicker."

He forced his lips against each other. He would not respond. He knew he would be sarcastic at best, obscene at worst. The process had been anything but fast. It had already been slow, dragged out, even tedious. They could say that an attorney would slow the process down, but it was already slow. They guaranteed it; they had kept the process slow. They had been intimidating him for too long — let them be intimidated for a while.

"My hiring a lawyer is non-negotiable. Do you have something else to say to me?"

Now she was silent. He figured she was trying to find some words to say. He waited. "Mr. Gunnarsen," she paused, it sounded to him like a deliberate hesitation, "I get the feeling," she stopped again. Whatever she wanted to say to him was making her nervous. "I get the feeling," she began again, "that you are not too comfortable with me."

That came as a surprise. If he told the truth in any form, no matter how tactfully he covered it, she would know. But he knew he could not lie, not now, not under these circumstances, and he could not keep silent. That would have the same impact as saying the words diplomatically.

"I suppose that is a fair assessment." He wanted to say Miss or Mrs., but it occurred to him he really did not know her marital status. "Ann, I am sorry if that hurts, but we have not really hit it off that well." He hoped that line would soften the blow.

"No need to apologize. In my work, I expect a certain amount of hostility. But you have been so helpful to this point that I really don't want to let things get out of hand because of me."

"My lawyer," he started to respond.

"No, no, no. I understand about your lawyer," she immediately interjected, "I am just concerned about my relationship with you. I don't want it to become a problem for you, for the agency," she sighed, "and for me."

He was confused. What is she saying? This is not a legal question. This sounds personal, is that right? "I am really not sure I understand you."

"No, I didn't think you would. Maybe, if you let me come over by myself or if you prefer we could go somewhere, like to a public restaurant. Let me buy, and let me explain."

"I have already eaten."

"Well, it does not have to be a restaurant, but someplace public that we could just talk, just you and me, in front of the world if you like so that I can explain myself."

Should he or shouldn't he? This was clearly nothing legal. She wanted to be sure it was public, so she was not hiding or trying to be secretive. But she wanted to explain herself, whatever that meant. He detected evil in her; maybe he was wrong. He should give her the benefit of the doubt. Wasn't that the good thing to do, the right thing to do, the Christian thing to do?

"Okay, I know a club...."

The club was well lit. He belonged to it and everyone knew him. He came here regularly to get away from things. He had brought clients, male and female here before, and nothing untoward could happen here. It was too public, and that is why he belonged and why he could safely bring people here.

The Ann Brown who showed up was not the social worker he knew. This Ann Brown was a woman. She was elegantly dressed. He did not usually note how a woman appeared, to his wife's constant dismay. But there was something about how Ann Brown appeared that was appealing, even sensual. And her perfume exuded a smell that put him at ease. His tensions upon agreeing to see her disappeared the moment she first arrived. He could not explain why, but he knew she calmed him by her presence.

She was all bubbly in her conversation. She was a skilled conversationalist. She never brought up anything provocative, and she ignored the whole family scenario. Ann Brown talked about the weather, the club, fashions, movies, books, anything she could think about, and anything he responded to. She was wonderful with jokes, friendly and simply easy to be around.

Surely he must have misjudged her. Here was the essence of grace and wit, good company, fine fellowship, and he perceived her as evil. He must be wrong. His sense had never failed him before — maybe this was a first.

She must have guessed what he thought because eventually she declared, "This is what I am, not the social worker. That is my job. I don't want you to see me as the enemy, even when I am doing my job. If you could just see me this way," she pleaded.

He did not know who to talk to about the evening. He was in the office of King McMasters again for some follow-up when King abruptly asked, "So did Ann Brown seduce you?"

"Excuse me, what are you talking about?"

"Ann Brown, when all else fails, suggests taking a client out somewhere, public, of course, so nothing can be said adversely. Then she puts on a show that any conman would be proud of. She is elegant. She is gracious. She is witty. She is simply great to be with, and it is all an act. Hell, and I use that word deliberately because if she isn't from hell there is no hell — she will do whatever it takes to get you to like her, to appreciate her, to become entwined by her. Some men and women she even takes to bed, if that is what is needed. I doubt if she bedded you."

"No."

"That answer tells me all. She did her routine on you, and you bought into it."

"It was all an act?" he couldn't believe he was defending her.

"Before you had this encounter, what did you think of her?"

"She was evil through and through."

"You were right, and she knew you felt thus about her. So she did her act. She has done it so many times with so many people I can't even number them any more. Here, read these."

McMasters threw a pile of papers across the desk they were sitting at. He looked down and read page after page describing last night as if the evening at the club had been wiretapped and videotaped. Somewhere on each page though was a different name than his. He counted twenty-seven different names, and when he looked up at McMasters, he saw King holding another pile of papers with other names on them.

"Do you want to see more?"

"No."

"I deliberately didn't tell you because I wanted you to see what you were up against. She is good, or maybe I should say she is clever at what she does. But really, she is evil and she will do whatever it takes for her evil to get into your psyche. You get sucked in by her and that is her gift from hell."

"How does she get away with it?"

"It works and the agency looks the other way. As long as it works and it is not illegal, they don't care."

"But what about the people she had sex with? I mean, surely that is illegal?"

"Nice try, but if I give you the papers that deal with sex, each client insists they brought it up and they made sure it had nothing to do with her work or anything that could be construed as influencing her opinions. She was so meticulous that at best the agency could not even file ethical charges against her. Personal lives, as long as they don't intrude on the work, are overlooked, and no one could ever say her professional opinions or her work were influenced by her personal relationships with certain clients. She could still make the client miserable. Every subsequent action with the client was correct, professional, exact and fully in accord with guidelines."

"How do you deal with someone like that?"

"Very carefully, and we document everything. It is your turn to write down exactly what happened. Even if we never use this or even if the agency ignores it, we have a paper trail that shows what she is and that may come in handy someday down the road."

And so he did.

Chapter 4

My Name Is Wanda Branski

My name is Wanda Branski. I am a retired elementary education teacher. I am a widow; my husband died eight years ago. We could not have children ourselves, so over the years, we have been short-term foster parents and emergency babysitters, usually through the Children's Affairs Division, but sometimes for other groups, agencies, even churches. I am a practicing Catholic, but I have handled children of all types of religions and some with no religion. I just make sure those children I am entrusted with are kept true to their beliefs. So if they have religious backgrounds, I make sure they go to their house of worship.

As a former elementary education teacher, I know young children. I was a master teacher, meaning I taught other teachers to teach, I helped mentor and evaluate teachers, I was the person the school referred to when educational questions arose about the children. Further, childhood development was my specialized field of endeavor when I did graduate work to ensure my continued certification as a teacher.

The kids just call me Granny Wanda, at my insistence. I want them to be comfortable with me; I want them to see me as a grandmotherly figure. Calling me Granny Wanda is the best tool I have found to make that happen.

I watch the kids. I play with the young ones. I feed them. I teach them inconspicuously. I make sure they feel my love and acceptance. I am a trained professional.

The above is the required preliminary material needed to make sense of what I am about to write concerning the Gunnarsens. Dr. Joan Prolewski approached me to do this. The agency agreed. I have let the Gunnarsens read the following. They have some quibbles, but overall they felt it was fair. If they had not said so, I would not let these impressions become part of the record. They would have been destroyed in my favorite paper shredder.

I type everything the old-fashioned way, on a good Remington electric typewriter. I don't use the computer at all, not even for email. In my line of work, it is too dangerous to use a computer, since nothing can be completely destroyed. Typing guarantees nothing can be traced back under any circumstances. If I had destroyed this, it would have been irrevocably lost.

Mr. Andrew Gunnarsen was understandably nervous when he first met me. That is a very typical reaction from a parent. The parent does not know anything about me. Hence, nervousness is a normal reaction. I accept that and try to set the parent at ease. Apparently it worked with Mr. Gunnarsen. After our first encounter, he was gracious and a true gentleman. In this day and age of incivility as the norm of human relations, it was refreshing to see a very civil person. He was always a pleasure to work with.

I would say we even became friends. He felt I was good to his children, that I was a grandmother to them. He appreciated that, even when I could tell he and the agency were having fights. He told me the day after he had hired the attorney that he had done so. I knew King McMasters, and he is a good man. I also knew attorney McMasters had some personal run-ins with the agency and was waiting to get even. I watched his children for a while when the agency felt his wife had acted inappropriately. He never forgave them, and I am sure he took the Gunnarsen's case simply for that reason.

"I told the attorney to leave you out of this," Mr. Gunnarsen said immediately after he told me about hiring the attorney. "You are too decent a person to be brought into this mess."

"Why thank you, Mr. Gunnarsen."

"Interestingly, when I mentioned your name, he said under no circumstances would he let anything happen to you. I think he knows you."

I could not reply, except to shrug my shoulders. After all, what I do is supposed to be confidential. Everything I say in here has been cleared by the proper authorities, including by King McMasters.

"Granny Wanda, I know it is not my business, but I really don't know how such a good person like you got involved with CAD."

"I know your concern about the agency, but I am here only to help out. I have a gift with children, and this makes it possible for me to help them out." I know it sounded vague, but how can I explain it? I do love children, and I am a gifted professional. I recognize this in myself. It is my gift to help children, and the agency made it possible for me to do so.

"You are a better person than I am," he remarked.

"I don't see it that way. I just want to help your children get through this mess."

He laughed. He always could laugh around me. "Mess is definitely the right word."

"I am just sorry we had to meet under these circumstances. You, Mr. Gunnarsen, are a remarkable man."

"If anybody else said that, I would think that person was buttering me up. But with you, I know it is sincere. Thank you."

I smiled and looked at his children playing in front of us. In our company, they were genuinely happy. I had finally earned Melissa's trust, and with her father nearby she was bubbling with joy.

"Daddy," she had overheard the conversation, "I'm glad you like Granny Wanda. She's a wonderful grandma."

"Yes, she is."

"Granny Wanda takes good care of us." Her sister rapidly nodded her assent. "She even takes us to church. I love church."

"I know you do, and I am grateful for Granny Wanda taking you."

"God loves me too, even when I am bad."

"Yes, he does. God definitely loves you."

"Maybe if I'm not so bad, God would let mommy come home."

"You are not being bad. You are being good. Mommy will be home soon. We just have to be patient."

I spoke up and said, "Melissa and Nicole, your mother will be coming to see you tomorrow, and I am sure you can tell her how much you love and miss her."

"Will the mean one be here too?"

Nicole, red-faced, turned to her sister and said angrily, "We can't say that."

Mr. Gunnarsen and I both knew to whom she was referring. It was no secret the children, especially Melissa, hated Ann Brown. Nicole was trying to be the diplomat, to ensure her mother would appear, even if that meant dealing with the despised Ann Brown.

Mr. Gunnarsen wanted to say something to assuage their fears, but he did not know who would be accompanying Mrs. Gunnarsen the next day. I did. The agency had already called me to tell me whom to expect. The agency always notified me twenty-four hours prior to a visit about every detail, including the caseworker accompanying Mrs. Gunnarsen.

"Jolene will be here with your mother."

"Yay!" screamed Melissa.

Nicole made her face into a rock and said solemnly, "Good!"

I could see Mr. Gunnarsen was relieved, but he knew better than to say anything provocative to the children. He contented himself with, "You and mommy will have a nice visit."

"But you won't be here, will you Daddy?" Nicole was sharp.

Before Mr. Gunnarsen could answer, Melissa jumped in, "You won't be here Daddy? That's not fair. I want you and mommy together. I don't care what anybody says. You and mommy will be here tomorrow!" Melissa was determined.

I tried to step in to help Mr. Gunnarsen, "I know it's not fair, but it's just for one day. Soon you will see mommy and daddy together always, so," and at that point before I could finish, Melissa went into a full tantrum.

She threw herself hard on the ground. She rolled in the dirt and grass and even some mud nearby. She howled and howled and howled some more. She sounded like a wounded dog. Most of her screams were incoherent but loud. I could make out the one line she repeated like a litany, "I want my mommy and daddy together!"

Mr. Gunnarsen was stunned. I do not believe he had ever seen his daughter throw such a tantrum before and clearly nothing like this had ever happened when I was watching her. Mr. Gunnarsen was going to intervene, but I stopped him. I told him we should let her get it out of her system. I wanted to intervene too. She was kicking. She was loud. I thought she might hurt herself. I could only imagine what the neighbors thought.

I do live in a dense neighborhood. This is not exactly isolated or wilderness, but true suburbia. Her tantrum was definitely attracting spectators. My neighbors were looking. They tried to be discrete at first, but eventually they did not disguise their curiosity. I knew if I intervened now her tantrums would come back to haunt me. I bit my lips and kept my hand in front of Mr. Gunnarsen.

"We dare not intervene!" I told a doubting Mr. Gunnarsen. "She would use this against us." He was tempted to act nonetheless.

"Trust me. If our time together has meant anything, trust me on this."

He calmed down. And as he calmed down, so did Melissa. Nicole just ignored her sister the whole time and went about playing. She knew how to deal with her sister in such a situation. We had to realize that Nicole knew best, child that she was. It is hard sometimes for adults to learn from children, but necessary.

Melissa came over to us and somehow stretched her body over both of us sitting there. Her head was on her father. Her legs were on me. The rest of her body was somewhere in between. And to both of our surprises, she promptly fell asleep in this awkward position.

Neither of us moved for ten minutes. For that same ten minutes, I felt I was at a Quaker meeting. We were that silent and still. My Quaker friends always felt I talked too much. They reminded me that even in the Catholic tradition, silence is honored. I admit I never liked going to monasteries or nunneries. I hated the silence. Yet I had Quaker friends, and if they could see that scene, they would have been proud of me.

After ten minutes, both Mr. Gunnarsen and I had had enough. We pointed with our hands and gently moved Melissa off of us. She slept through the whole procedure. We quietly moved away. When we were at what we thought was a safe distance, we talked again.

"It worked," I muttered.

"Yeah, but I don't know if I am going to walk right for a week after that." He stretched his arms and his legs. He twisted his neck. He was sore.

I wasn't. I understood though what he felt like. When they sprawl on you, children can leave you with aches and pains, even though they did not mean it. It had happened to me before.

"I think I'll wait a bit to see if she is going to wake up before I take her home."

"I think that would be a good idea." The neighbors by now had retreated. I expected though that later in the evening, some of them would either call or stop by and try to get me to talk about what happened. I knew I would have to come up with some excuse or another. I always did when something went awry with the children. But the neighbors tried to believe me, though they were not always successful. They were good neighbors and they trusted me too.

Melissa was obviously out for the count. The tantrum took its toll on her. Mr. Gunnarsen waited an hour before he finally picked her up, put her in the car and drove off. She slept the whole time, he told me later, and she did not get up until the next morning. Of course, as I was told, she ate a large breakfast — large by any standards. She was ravenously hungry.

"I ate three bowls of cereal and I was still hungry. Daddy made me some scrambled eggs. I ate all of them. So Daddy made me two sausages and three pieces of toast. I ate all of them. I even drank my milk and four big glasses of orange juice. I am still hungry. Can you get me something to eat?"

By my estimation, she finished eating only a half-hour before, but I started making pancakes. Nicole saw them and ran into the other room. She wanted nothing to do with more food. I made the pancakes one at a time, expecting to stop after each one. She ate ten before she quit. And she drank apple juice, grape juice, cranberry juice and another glass of orange juice. I have never seen anything like it, and I hope I never see it again.

What was most amazing was that it did not even slow her down. She did not head to the bathroom. She never showed signs of an upset stomach, nor did she show so much as a pound of that on her body thereafter. She must have some metabolism. When she got up from the table, she went playing at full steam. I could almost swear she was like an old coal train, just keep putting that fuel in and the train keeps on chugging along.

It was a Saturday. About twice a month, Mr. Gunnarsen needed to be out of town on weekends for business purposes. On those weekends, naturally I took his children to church, but also I had the children at my house overnight. He would usually return on Sunday evening, but it could be late depending on when he returned from his trip. The agency, of course, knew his schedule and kept a particular interest in his trips. Indeed, it was decided that when possible, Mrs. Gunnarsen could visit the children at my home when Mr. Gunnarsen was not there. Especially now that Mr. Gunnarsen had retained an attorney, the agency wanted to be aware of everything that was happening when the children met their mother. And they did not want the distraction of Mr. Gunnarsen offering his interpretation of events.

I admit I am surprised the preceding sentence was not edited out by the agency. I know with Dr. Prolewski, the agency insists on editorial control of what she writes. She admitted as such to me and the agency made it a point to tell me that was part of its contract with her. The agency has never edited what I say or write for any purposes. I always wondered why, until I found out from a friend who knows someone in the agency. The agency has a difficult time finding foster parents and babysitters and the like, and the last time they insisted on editorial control, they lost almost all of their "parents" in a very successful "strike." The agency left without anyone to watch the children quickly gave in, and the issue has never resurfaced. When I started with the agency, it was already a dead issue as far as the agency was concerned.

I can say the agency has not always been happy with my assessments, especially of the agency, but they have been happy with my results with the children, and thus they have never said anything to me. I guess they tolerate my criticisms because they value my work and the incredible amount of time I have given them. I am available on weekends and not everyone working for the agency will watch the youth on weekends.

Ann Brown came in first. She always did. Jolene Raycox would pick up Mrs. Gunnarsen, while Ann Brown was here first to ensure everything was satisfactory for the upcoming visit. If Ann Brown saw any problems, she had the authority to cancel. She would just pick up her cell phone and call Jolene Raycox and tell her not to pick up Mrs. Gunnarsen or even once to return Mrs. Gunnarsen. Yes, one time, I could see the car with Jolene Raycox and Mrs. Gunnarsen approach and then quickly veer off and not return. I turned and saw Ann Brown on the phone shaking her head and I could read her lips saying no emphatically over and over again.

To this day, I do not know why Ann Brown turned Jolene Raycox and Mrs. Gunnarsen away. I do know that the children were terrible that day, and I had to deal with them. Melissa was typically the worst. She screamed at me. She told me she hated me. She saw Ann Brown leaving and screamed at her. For the first time, Melissa actually ran up to Ann Brown and hit her and called her the b-word. I can't say it. I come from a different generation, where curse words were considered impolite and unacceptable. Now it is casual and everyone uses them. Even a little child like Melissa knows them. What are we coming to?

I had to physically restrain Melissa. Ann Brown actually smiled and seemed to be enjoying Melissa's anger. She even winked at Melissa. Melissa, in response, began what I would call a litany. To anything Ann Brown now said or did, Melissa simply said, "Evil, evil." And Ann Brown kept winking, kept smiling and even made it a point to say Melissa's name gently. Melissa repeated the litany. The back and forth between Ann Brown and Melissa became bizarre, in my impression. Ann Brown could have left quickly and avoided the confrontation or at least most of it, but she deliberately stayed, and dare I say it, egged Melissa on.

When Ann Brown finally did leave that day, Melissa was inconsolable. I had to spend the rest of the day doing nothing but calming her and Nicole. I had to reassure them, but they did not believe my reassurance. It was not a good day, and I had to be grandmotherly because nothing less would ease the disappointment.

This day, though, Ann Brown came and looked around and did not once pick up her cell phone. That meant the girls would see their mother. Thank God. The girls would be well-behaved and genuinely happy afterwards. Of course, Melissa would still be sad for a short time when she knew she could not stay with her mother, but that would wear off and she would be content.

Jolene Raycox got out of the car first. That was also part of the ritual. Mrs. Gunnarsen could not get out of the car until after Jolene Raycox gave her permission. Even with the children next to the car as they were now, Mrs. Gunnarsen had to wait for the final clearance by Ann Brown and Jolene Raycox before she could greet them. This was always the hardest time on Mrs. Gunnarsen. I could see it in her face. The children were filled with happy anticipation, but Mrs. Gunnarsen did not know whether she would be able to exit the car and be with her children. She had anxiety and despair written all over her face.

After consulting with Ann Brown, Jolene Raycox opened the door for Mrs. Gunnarsen. The relief on Mrs. Gunnarsen's face was palpable. She quickly wrapped her arms around her children and smiled. She never smiled until that moment; her anxiety and despair so dominated her before this moment.

"How are my girls? Mommy loves you and misses you both!"

The girls at virtually the same time told their mother how much they loved her, how much they missed her, how much they were glad to see her, how much they wanted her to stay. I had not noticed others' reactions before, but since I had seen this scene many times previously, I unconsciously turned to look at Ann Brown. She was frowning and her face was ugly. I hate to say that about any person, but it was true. Her face had turned ugly. It was distorted. It was as if she had been to one of those Halloween make-up shops, wherein someone had spent hours remaking her face into one of those old Hollywood monsters. Of course, it was a face of her own instantaneous making, but a make-up artist would nonetheless have been impressed. A director would have cast her in a horror movie on the spot.

I must have stared too long and too intensely. She somehow sensed my stare, peripherally glanced at me and immediately resumed her normal, bland face. She did not say a word to me, nor did she physically acknowledge me. For the rest of the time with the children, she simply observed the scene clinically as a good professional would do.

Mrs. Gunnarsen was so engrossed in the children that she never picked up on my exchange with Ann Brown. Jolene Raycox also did not pick up on the scene. Thus, it is my word against Ann Brown's, who has since denied any knowledge of the aforementioned incident. She can deny it all she wants. I have had nightmares ever since about Ann Brown's face. If I never believed in the power of dreams before, I do now. Many times I have awakened horribly in the middle of the night having seen that face. It still scares me and yet terribly holds me in my worst nightmares. I cannot get away from that face and my consciousness forces me to awaken. It is the only way I can escape that face.

Mrs. Gunnarsen kissed her children numerous times. She hugged them. She held their little hands. She swung their hands as if she were playing a game with them. She kept repeating how much she loved them and maybe soon she would be back with them. I quickly returned my gaze to Ann Brown, but Ann Brown remained professional. She did not change her facial appearance.

I have been asked repeatedly since what that facial response of Ann Brown meant. I said I could only speculate and I am sure such an opinion would not be legally acceptable. Nonetheless, I was given permission to speculate. I pointed out that from my professional background, such a facial expression often meant a personal boundary was being violated. I was told that was too clinical, even ambiguous, and I needed to clarify what I meant for a non-clinician.

Very well, I said, it was as if Ann Brown had some sort of claim on the children, a claim that was being ignored or run roughshod over by Mrs. Gunnarsen. Mrs. Gunnarsen *is* the children's mother! It seems strange to me that Ann Brown could have any superior claim to the children than their mother.

The remainder of the time with the children was uneventful. Indeed, nothing like this transpired in subsequent visits. Mrs. Gunnarsen followed all the rules and acted appropriately. She was a loving mother, a caring mother, a compassionate mother. I too feel with Mr. Gunnarsen that the agency's reaction was an unnecessary overreaction. No doubt she did strike Melissa inappropriately, but the agency treated her as if she had come close to killing the child and was still a threat to the child's survival. I never saw any indication of such behavior.

In light of that event, I must now wonder how much attention the agency paid to Ann Brown originally, or how much of an impact Ann Brown had on making the original assessment. I have been foster parent, nanny, grandmother, babysitter to authenticated serious child abusers. I have seen how the children looked and how the children reacted to the abuser. I have seen how the children reacted to the agency and to me. In all of my years of caring for these weakest and most abused little ones, I have never seen the love and caring between mother and children so evident between Mrs. Gunnarsen and her children. There was nothing to indicate Mrs. Gunnarsen was a terrible abuser, a serial abuser, or anything but a mother who had overreacted and should have been treated with compassion and dignity.

They drove off, Mrs. Gunnarsen saying as she said every time she left, "Maybe, next time, God willing!" She would then bow her head and close her eyes for a few seconds, no doubt praying that God would be willing. The children inevitably followed their mother's lead. And then the cars would drive off. The children would start crying. They would come over to me, and I would hug them, embrace them, hold on to them. And their crying stopped. They would resume their normal activities, usually playing, but occasionally their eyes would surreptitiously peer in the direction whence the car departed. It was as if they could wish the car and their mother back, and this whole episode would be over. But of course, it wasn't yet.

Chapter 5

Angela Gunnarsen's Tape

I am recording myself now. Yeah, the tape recording is working well. I just feel the need to start keeping my own record of what is going on. Maybe it will help, maybe it will be therapeutic. But I don't know if I will tell Dr. Prolewski about these tapes. I know she felt I ought to keep some sort of record, a journal perhaps, to follow my own psyche, whatever that means. But I am not a journal person. I don't like to write things down.

So here I am talking into this machine, and no doubt knowing I will have to change the tape occasionally as it gets near the end. I will try to say something appropriate when that happens, so I don't get sidetracked when I have to start again on the next tape. Oh yeah, of course there are two sides to the tape, so I will just have to turn it over first. But be that as it may, I have bought a batch of tapes. How many I will use only God knows; I surely don't.

I have been able to see Andrew apart from the children for some time now. Thank God. It was difficult for him the first time, and I admit I was still angry with him. But I know if he hadn't acted like he did, the children would have been gone from both of us for who knows how long. And my separation was better than losing the children indefinitely. It hurts, God knows it hurts. There are times I really want to strangle him, but he was in an impossible situation and he did what he could do and it was necessary, right and accurate.

Andrew would laugh if he heard me saying that. Even when we were in total agreement about some issue, he would always wonder if I fully agreed with him. He just could never be sure about me. He has always been so precise, so definite, so...I don't know the word. He was very easy to read. I always knew where he stood on any issue. He did not waffle. He was very thorough, very specific. And he was meticulous, marshaling his case comprehensively. He should have been a lawyer, but he always told me that was his business training. In the business world, if people did not know where you stood and why you stood there, you were lost. Your business associates would not trust you, much less deal with you, and you could forget about the customers. The customers needed you to be that way.

I guess that was why I never got into business. I had to analyze every matter from all possible angles. I could never be so definite. Indeed, I could change my position several times before acting, and I never held my position as imperative. I live for complexity, ambiguity. Yeah, and now my living for complexity and ambiguity has brought me to this point. Now I can at least understand him, and now I can accept his actions. Yeah, he really would laugh at my saying that to him.

I love him and I know he loves me. The rascal, the third time after I saw him alone, he bought me a dozen roses and a diamond pendant. I didn't know he had it in him, but I cried when he gave me those gifts. He told me he knew they couldn't make up for what was happening to me, but he wanted me to know he loved me and he felt I had earned these. I deserved these. Yeah, he used the words "earned" and "deserved." I know Dr. Joan (I do call her by her first name occasionally, she really wants me to) finally did phone him and gave him a brief overview of what was happening in our sessions, with my permission, of course.

The agency reluctantly agreed to the good doctor calling. Andrew had hired the attorney by then and they were afraid everything and anything said could be used by the attorney against them. And they really did not like the attorney Andrew hired. He apparently is their worst nightmare. Good for Andrew! But Dr. Joan felt it was necessary and they could find no real good reason to deny her calling, other than the attorney issue. And the agency I gather knew that would not fly, so they authorized it, reluctantly.

So hey, the roses were beautiful, wonderful and they made me feel good. The diamond pendant I wear every day. I see it as a sign of reunification. It will happen. And my husband and I had one of the best nights ever after he gave me those gifts. I guess I am an old romantic and can be seduced still by my wonderful husband. He is still a romantic, and so am I. God bless him.

Oh, it is time to turn over this tape. Okay I am back in business. I just hope I know what I am doing taping myself. It would be just like old Richard Nixon or Lyndon Johnson if these tapes got out and they were used against me. Well, I don't care. This is who I am, and if they get out, people will just have to judge me as they see fit. I can only hope if they do that people will hear me and give me the benefit of the doubt. All I know is I have to have an outlet, and this is it for me.

Hallelujah, the agency is going to let me have a sleepover with my kids! I feel like a teenager again. Mom let me sleep over with certain friends, and it was fun. Of course, sleepover is a relative term. I really did not get much sleep as we were up most of the night talking. I imagine it will be the same with Melissa and Nicole. Andrew won't be there. The agency knows his business requires him to be out of town and they have approved my being with the kids alone for the first time. I gather from Doctor Joan that this will be the test that leads me to reclaiming my daughters and finally being reconciled with my family.

In other words, friends and neighbors, if I do this right, it will be only a brief matter of time when all of us can be in the house together. Thank God, I can be mother again, in fact, as well as in name.

Well hey, look at this. Here come my sweeties now. They are being driven by ding and dong, better known as *the social workers*. My enemies approach. I better turn this thing off before they see it, or I am sure they would find a way to take it from me and maybe even use it against me. Click!

I am recording again now that they are gone. It took about a half-hour to get them out of here. They gave me the full lecture on appropriate behavior, on agency policy and how the children were to contact them if anything went amiss. Also, they reminded me that the children would be thoroughly debriefed (their word, as if kids could be debriefed) in the morning. Dr. Joan would also be meeting with me immediately thereafter. Indeed, Dr. Joan Prolewski would be coming to my house and interview me here. The children would be interviewed elsewhere, meaning not in my presence. If all went satisfactorily (their word again, not one I would use), my moving back into the house would occur in a relatively short amount of time (they did not define relatively short amount of time, but I guess it meant in a couple of weeks after several more sleepovers).

Well, I will show them. I am going to be the good mother, the loving mother, the controlled mother. They won't find anything suspect in me as a result of tonight. I guarantee you that. Amen!

Sweet Nicole is fascinated by the tape recorder. She wants to hear my voice so I say, "Hi Nicole," into the recorder and play it back to her. She asks me if she can speak into it and hear her voice. I, of course, say sure. "I love you, Mommy." I play it back and she smiles.

She is now watching me as I am talking. She laughs at me and then comes up to me, hugs me and leans up close to the microphone. "Mommy, you know Ann Brown touched us all over."

"What do you mean, Nicole?"

"On TV, they would say she fondled us, petted us, touched our privates."

"Do you know what you are saying, Nicole?"

"Of course, Mommy. She did it first on the night when you left home after you hit Melissa. We were taken upstairs and she was touching us through our clothes when Daddy came upstairs.

She stopped before Daddy got in the room. She has done it many times since. She even took off Melissa's clothes and rubbed her body all over Melissa just two days ago. She doesn't do that to me. She says she really loves Melissa."

"Nicole, you are not making this up, sweetie?"

"No, Mommy. Ask Melissa. Why do you think Melissa calls Ann Brown evil?"

"Melissa, come here. Melissa, you are running away from me. I love you. Melissa, please come here. You are shaking your head, but you have stopped. And Melissa, are you crying? Did Ann Brown do those things to you?"

"I can't tell you, Mommy. Ann Brown would be angry and I would never get you back as my mommy."

"What? I can't believe my ears. This can't be happening. This can't be true. Nicole, what does Melissa mean?"

"She said if we tell you, you can't be our mother ever again. Melissa believes her, I don't. And I thought you knew. That is why you got us tonight, I said or they would never let mommy have us."

"No, I got you because I am getting better and we are going to be together always very soon."

"Oh. I shouldn't have told you."

"Yes, you should have. Melissa, please tell me the truth."

"Nicole is right. I hate her, Mommy. She is evil, evil, evil. She is evil, evil, evil. Good people don't do that to children, Mommy."

"No, they don't."

The tape is ending. I am going to put another tape on. This has to be recorded. Okay, testing. Yeah, it is working. Where's the phone? I have lived in this house and now I can't remember where the phone is. It must be the shock. Melissa and Nicole are just looking at me. They seem to be waiting expectantly.

"Girls, I need to make some phone calls real quick. Do you know where the phone is?"

Nicole is taking my hand and she just walks me right to it on the wall by the banister. I remember Andrew's cell phone number. I am dialing it and over some static I hear his voice.

"I am sorry to bother you, Andrew, but I think you need to hear this. Nicole, would you tell your Daddy what you just told me? I am going in the kitchen. Just call me when Daddy wants to speak to me, okay?"

I just gave her the phone and ran into the kitchen. I am sitting down at the kitchen table. It is one of those modern glass jobs on black metal legs. I am looking into it and can see my reflection as in a mirror though not as clearly. But I am seeing clearly enough and what I see is my face frightened, fearful, scared, terrified. My hand is shaking on the table. I can't control it. That bitch, that evil, damnable bitch. I hope she goes to hell. She's a pedophile.

And here I am the one who is supposed to be a danger to my children. Hypocrite! I wouldn't be surprised if she arranged to have the kids taken out just so she could get to them. That is the perfect position for a pedophile, isn't it? Use the cover of child abuse to gratify yourself sexually with kids. They can't fight you. They can't talk about it. They just put up with it and then you're gone to the next group of kids.

My God, it is amazing Nicole even told me. Melissa wouldn't. But hey, she mentioned TV. Somewhere, she must have seen something on TV. But where, how?

Wanda Branski! I wonder if she suspected. Sure, she would have guessed, and trying to find some way to get through looked for a children's program on that and put it on while the girls were watching. I'll ask Wanda next time I see her, but I am willing to bet that is what happened. And the program got through to Nicole. My sweet Nicole. The one who stopped me from beating Melissa has now stopped Ann Brown. She may not be aware but this is going to rebound on the agency. They will get a piece of their own medicine if I know Andrew like I know Andrew. He will get in touch with that lawyer immediately.

"Mommy, Daddy wants to talk to you." That is Nicole calling me.

"Andrew?"

"I am calling my attorney as soon as I get off the phone. Don't do anything until you hear from him or me. Understood?"

"Yes, dear."

"I love you. One of us will get back to you shortly. Bye."
Click.

He's calling his attorney King McMasters right now. The
girls are looking at me, waiting for me to say or do something
and here I am talking out loud to this tape. They are not too sure
what to think. "Nicole, you are very brave, and I am glad you
told me. I am glad you knew what Ann Brown was doing was
wrong. Did you see that on TV somewhere?"

"Yes, Mommy. Granny Wanda lets us watch TV, and she
told us she had a show she really liked and wanted us to see it
too. The TV show showed little kids like us talking about bad
people touching them, fondling them, playing with their genitals
as they said on the show. And many times on the show we were
told to tell somebody we loved, and so I told you."

"I thought Granny Wanda might have shown you that
program and I am glad she did. I love you both so much. You,
come here. Let me put my arms around you, just like this.
Mommy is going to cry now, okay?"

"Can I cry too, Mommy?" That is Nicole.

"Yes, of course, you can."

"Can I cry, too?"

"You know you can, Melissa."

(*Note: Crying is now heard on the tape for several minutes
and then the tape is turned off.*)

Chapter 6

Selections from Ann Brown's Diary

MAY 2

I saw a goddess today. Her name is Melissa Gunnarsen. She is the most beautiful child I have ever seen. I must have her. She must be mine. Her mother had abused her, and her father wasn't even around. They don't deserve her. They call her hyperactive. What do they know? I will take care of her. I will protect her. I will possess her. I will love her. She will be my love child.

I have already started to claim her. She is so soft, so tender. Of course, she has a sister, Nicole, and I cannot let sibling rivalry enter into the picture. Melissa must be mine, but Nicole I will embrace too in order that Melissa may belong to me forever. If only their father had not entered at the moment of purest embrace, we could all be in heaven now. They would know I was made for them, and that Melissa is to be my desire fulfilled and her childhood satisfied. Nicole will come to understand in time.

I have waited years for this moment. I went into Children's Affairs Division dreaming of children, especially little girls who need love, the pure physical love of a woman who would accept them and help them to know what love is really about. I have touched other little girls before, but they were passing fantasies, a momentary pleasure in my pursuit of the perfect love child. I fell in love with Melissa the moment I saw her. I knew she was to be the one I wanted. I knew she was to be the one I lived for. Melissa, darling, you belong to me and I belong to you. Come, let us grow in love together!

My reputation is so phenomenal I can do anything I want at the division. They trust me implicitly. They believe in me explicitly. I have commendations filling my drawers and decorating my walls. I was the ideal employee, the perfect CAD. Ha, ha, even I joke about the agency's stupid initials. It has been the butt of jokes and barbs by so many, why not me? The agency will never know anyway. I have modeled the agency. I have been professional to the core. I have been precise and exacting. My documentation has been unimpeachable. I know what I am doing.

But now I am going to have my way. Melissa Gunnarsen, my dream, my goddess, you belong to me. I will do whatever it takes to get you, to possess you, to love you, to have you in my arms and ultimately in my bed. I can manipulate the agency any way I want. That mother really should just have some counseling and help in parenting. I expect she is no continual abuser. But that will not be the official line. With her out of the way, I will have easier access to the children, and especially my love, my future, my Melissa.

MAY 11

Oh yes, it was everything I dreamed it would be. All my years of touching were nothing compared to this. It was orgasmic. It was perfection. Our naked bodies intertwined as I embraced her, held her, loved her. And I knew then this is what I was made for, this is who I am, this is my life. Everything else was but preparation for this moment.

Melissa, Melissa, Melissa! Oh I will say that name to the heavens. Child of love, child of my love, child to love and beloved, Melissa. Yes, Melissa. You and I are bound together for eternity. You have made me a woman, my child. You have given me life, my child.

And perfection had to be interrupted by Nicole's looks. I could see her anger. I could see her fear. I could see even her disgust. Oh, Nicole, if you could only understand love like Melissa and I do, you would not object but would rather cheer! So I had to tell her not to talk. I had to give Nicole the fear conversation. Do you want to lose your mommy and daddy forever? If you talk, you will. I will see to it. I have taken you away from your mommy already. You know I can do it forever and I can take you away from your daddy too. You don't want me to do that, do you, Nicole?

She shook her head and I could see I had won. Fear always overcomes disgust. Fear always prevents anger from taking over. Fear dictates life. Nicole, Melissa is my life or you lose everything, do you understand? And to show Nicole I meant business, I stripped her right there and caressed her body parts, all over.

Do you want your parents to know about you now? What would they think of a little girl being touched all over by a woman? Why, they would not think much of you. They would not like you at all. Why, they would hate you because you are evil. They would know you are no good. Do good girls do what you just did? Of course not. And if you tell, you will never be loved again by your parents. They will hate you. They will get rid of you forever. And even if somehow they didn't, I would see to it that they had nothing to do with you ever again. You know I can do it.

I saw the fear. I saw the fear become incarnate. I saw the fear live and breathe and possess her, and I knew I had won. Nicole would never talk and Melissa would be mine.

JUNE 1

They arrested one of us today. I couldn't avoid hearing about it. It was in the newspapers, on the radio, on the TV too. To quote their garbage, "Pedophile arrested. Under indictment

‹John Helgeson›

for allegedly molesting many children. Prosecutor to seek maximum punishment. Mayor praises police for their work in getting the scum off the streets. Children will be safer."

They don't understand. They call us evil. They call us criminals. They give us a name. They brand us like murderers. They don't understand love and our special need to love. They don't realize that we need love like everyone else. We just love children. We are adults who believe the purest and best love is an adult loving a child physically, completely.

I need little girls. Hey, at least the Man-Boy Love organization is out there fighting the fight that we need to make. If they would only read their history, they would know that in the classical world, men were expected to have boys as their lovers first before they graduated to women, if they graduated to women. And those boys were trained to love by men first before they could move on. Is it any different with women and girls?

But they won't understand. Their parents are shocked, sickened and demand we be imprisoned. If they would only understand, they would give us their children for our pleasure, for our love, because they know we need their children physically to satisfy our natural desires. They should have children for us to love, to embrace, to become our means of sexual satisfaction. They satisfy themselves sexually; yet, they dare to deprive us sexually. So what if we need children? There is no difference between our sexual needs and theirs.

They call us evil. They think we are perverted. They call us incapable of understanding a child. They think we ruin a child by our taking them. No, we are fulfilling them. We are showing them what life is all about. And they sue the good priests who were doing what they should do to those children. They want to imprison them too. They even let the convicts in prison kill them. Hey, it is not my fault or theirs so many of the people in prison were quote 'sexually abused by an adult as a child' unquote. And those prisoners think they will get vindication by killing off some of us.

We need to teach people that what happened to them was not bad but good. All sex is good and the sooner it starts the

‹*77*›

better. If it happens to you by an adult, consider it an act of love. Those psychologists who say a child can't handle it don't understand. The psychologists need to teach children that this act was wonderful, good, necessary and not something to get crazy about or become a criminal for.

If I had my way ultimately, I would teach everybody that there is really no evil, no wrong, no immorality, just societal prejudices and needs. And the sooner we get rid of God the better. The people who believe in God believe in morality. The people who believe in God believe there are things that are evil or wrong. We have to get rid of God too. Only what we want and what we need should count.

Of course, I won't say that to anybody. They wouldn't understand. They never understand. I haven't been to a church in years, but if I could I would go to one of those churches served by the "molesting" priest. He would understand. He would know the type of religion we need. He would get beyond some sort of moral God. He would help people to see that the most important aspect of life is sex, as Freud once said. Everything and everybody has to deal with sex. We are sexual beings from birth and I just want us to live that. In the old Biblical times, there was a religion called Baalism based on sex. The Greeks and Romans worshipped Venus, the goddess of love. They recognized the power of sex. They even went so far as to declare Bacchus a god and they had orgies in his name. They knew sex was really the purest religion of all.

But no. They want to imprison my brothers and sisters. They want to call us criminals. They want to see us as perverse. They want to see us as evil. They want their God to let us have it. They don't see that we are all products of natural forces, and sex is the most primal, most basic natural force of all. We have to have sex period.

Give me my Melissa. She was made for me. Forget law. Forget morality. Forget psychology. Forget anything but me and my need for sex with Melissa. I am woman and I need a little girl as my physical lover, and I will have her despite what anybody might say. She is mine and I will do whatever it takes to have her. I defy the law. I will lie, cheat, steal, even kill, if necessary to have her. She is mine. I work for an agency that makes it easy for me to do what I need to do. There are always places for my brothers and sisters to go, to work for.

Those priests had found their place because they knew their bishops would let them get away with it, since they were priests and the bishops would do anything to protect and keep their priests. But now that place is out of bounds. My brothers will have to find a new secret outlet until the secret is allowed. It is easier for me here, since I can hide in plain sight and I can use the law to help me.

What power. What a gift. I am CAD, you can't do anything to me. You can't stop me. I am above the law. I decide people's fates and if I decide I want a girl as my reward, no let me say my price, to save the parents from their deserved punishment, so be it. The parents beat their children. All parents do. I intervene. I stop them for the sake of society, and I then show what real love is. Not the parents' version of it. So what if they had children? They can't show them love; I can. I will. Sex is love; love is sex. A boy needs to learn to love a man physically, and a girl needs to love a woman physically. That is love, and we who they dare to call *pedophiles* love purely.

JUNE 10

Melissa was afraid of me today. I could see the fear in her eyes. That was good. Fear is my best gift. I induce fear. I live for fear. I want her to fear me and know that she will be punished if she does not fear me. I will be god to her, and she will be afraid of me, totally and completely. Then she will do whatever I want her to do, and oh, the plans I have for her.

Ha, ha, ha. I will be in control. I will be her lord and master. She will be my love slave. She will fear me. Yes, fear is a good thing. Terrifying a child is a wonderful thing. Controlling a situation to get my own way is right. Lying like I have done to ensure Melissa belongs to me is necessary and good. As long as my pleasure is met, there is no evil. Anything I do for myself is right and proper. Melissa exists for me, and if fear is what it takes, lying is what it takes, control is what it takes, I will do that and more.

If the father gets in the way, I will do whatever it takes to keep him out of the picture. I can be very persuasive. I can be anything anybody wants me to be to make them heed and give in to me. If they want sex, I will provide it. If they want company, I will be the sweetest she-devil imaginable. I am good. I am seductive. I am temptress. I am in control.

Whatever I want I get. I want Melissa and there is nothing I would not do to ensure it happens. I will find a way, some very logical, practical, bureaucratic way to ensure she comes to me and stays with me. Maybe when her mother is around I will hit Melissa and leave marks and then blame it on her mother. Who will they believe? Me, of course. Not that damned abusing mother or that absent father. No, I will help out as only I can help out and no one will be the wiser. Melissa and Nicole are too afraid to do anything.

I have the agency at my fingertips. They slobber over me. Good dogs, do what Ann tells you to do. For the sake of me, there is nothing wrong. To satisfy me, nothing is unacceptable; nothing is out of bounds. The cops know me. The courts know me. I have made myself known so well and in such convincing ways that everyone believes me the greatest, the saintliest. What assholes!

I have what I want and I will keep her.

UNDATED

I don't think I will date anything anymore. Not after seeing that Wanda Branski looking at me. My face must have given me away. No matter. One slip-up. I better watch myself now. I could see she didn't know what to make of me thereafter. I think I have given her the slip, but I have to find some way to get the kids out of there.

Maybe now is the time to recommend sending the children home. Maybe now they will spend some time with their mother, when father is away, and I will be able to intervene. You abused your child again. What are you talking about? Look at the marks you put on her. You did this. You are finished with this child forever. Your husband is too, since he couldn't or wouldn't stop you, especially as he was away for the day. He should have known better. We will just have to take the children away. We will separate them, and I will be put in charge of Melissa. It will work. I guarantee it will work.

The agency will believe that crap. They exist to believe that crap. The truth, or anything beyond their simple minds, they can't believe. A child is abused period. There are no gray areas. There are no mitigating circumstances. There are only children abused, and parents who cannot control themselves lose their children, period. It is such a wonderful system for a person like me.

Yes, I knew I would get my love if I stayed in this business long enough, and now I will. I am great. I am the best. I get what I want any time I want and nobody can stop me. Nobody!

Chapter 7

Telephone Conversation Between Andrew Gunnarsen And Attorney King McMasters

(Note: One requirement of being represented by Attorney King McMasters is allowing all telephone calls by clients to be recorded. It is included in the signed contract between the lawyer and the client. The following is a transcript of one such conversation. The office receptionist's comments have been deleted.)

"Hello, Andrew. What's up?"

"Ann from hell has molested my daughters."

Gasping. "Am I hearing what I think you just said?"

Angrily, "I just got off the phone with my wife and my daughters, and both girls have told me that Ann Brown has been sexually molesting them since day one. Without knowing it, I managed to stop her from fully going at it the first night because I was so angry and ran upstairs to see her. And she told me she was just interviewing the kids privately. Yeah, she needed privacy all right, the privacy to sexually molest two little girls and take advantage of the situation, and…"

Interrupting, "Hold on a minute, Mr. Gunnarsen. Back up a second. The children are with their mother now, is that right?"

"Yes, sir."

"Now, I don't want you to take this the wrong way, but as a lawyer, your lawyer, I have to ask this next question. Just don't yell at me for asking the question. Promise?"

"I suppose."

"How do you know the children are not being manipulated by their mother?"

Calmly, "I expected precisely that question, and I pride myself on being fully prepared for objections in my business. If I could not, I would not be in business long. But to answer your question, I called Wanda Branski before I called you. I told my wife I would call you first after talking to her, but I had to be sure it was not manipulation, so I called Wanda Branski. She had picked it up from the children first before they told their mother. They had told her, and actually it was Wanda who pushed the children to tell somebody. That somebody happened to be my wife."

"Holy shit. Halleluiah! We may just have the asshole once and for all, and the agency is...I am sorry, excuse my language."

"It's okay. I am rather angry myself."

"You don't sound like it; you actually sound rather calm."

"In my business, Mr. McMasters, calm is essential in a storm, and this clearly qualifies as a storm."

"You're right about that. I will need to call Wanda myself. She and I go way back as you know, so I will get all the nice dirty details from her."

"I told my wife not to do anything until you or I got back to her. What do I do about that?"

"After you hang up with me, call her right back and tell her I will shortly be in touch with her. Let me see, yes, here's your home phone number where your wife is now. So yes, I will call her and tell her what is next. But don't hang up now, I need to explain to you what happens now and hereafter."

"Okay."

"After I talk to Wanda, I will call your wife and tell her to lock the doors until I get over there. I will be going to your house. She is to let me in but nobody else. From your house, I will talk to the children for a few minutes in front of your wife to get their basic story. Then I will call the agency and tell them what I have learned. I will also tell them that if they come over to the house then or tomorrow or until they have talked to me I will hit them with a very public, nasty lawsuit and for good measure, I will go directly to the media with the story."

Nervously, "Is that really necessary?"

"Yes and no. The threat is all that is necessary. Nothing will become public now. They don't dare let it. It would be suicide for the agency, and they will know it. They may be bureaucrats and nasty bureaucrats at that over at CAD, but they are not stupid."

Silence as each waits for the other and then, "Is that all?"

"Oh no, Mr. Gunnarsen, not at all. I will be contacted by the agency's staff, including their lawyer, demanding to allow the children to be interviewed."

Unbelieving, "Demanding?"

"Yes, they will demand. Damn, they will even use the word. They will throw every legal argument into the mix and even threaten some court order if I don't comply. But the fact is I intend to comply, but I will insist on a court stenographer taking down a legal transcript of the hearing. That way they can't weasel out of anything. Of course, I know a judge, M. Edward Winthrop by name, who will be more than glad to order just such. The agency got to his family once. Did I ever tell you the agency loves to go after prominent people?"

Interrupting, "Please go on with what happens hereafter."

"Sorry. You just don't know how happy this makes me. And I can get all of my Ann Brown files into play legally. Anyway, the children will be interviewed, and we will have Ann Brown and the agency by the balls."

"Is that all?"

"No. From this moment on, your kids are free of the agency, your wife is free of the agency, and you, Mr. Andrew

Gunnarsen, are free of the agency. They can't touch you, your wife or your children! CAD and Ann Brown are dead, and there will be no resurrection for them. To save their butts, they will do anything, and the first of our demands will be to drop this case immediately. They will have no choice. The irony of what has happened to your children is what will save them."

Quietly, "'What you meant for evil, God has used for good.' I believe that is what the Bible says."

"Joseph. I read it too. Of course it could also be Esther."

"Who knows, maybe you have been put in this position for just this situation?"

"Well, at least we're both on the same pages, Andrew. Evil does get caught up. I have prayed for this day for years. And right now I just want to be God's avenging angel and give them the hell they have long deserved, if you are willing to let me."

"What are you saying?"

Softly but firmly. "You and I have been given the rare opportunity to reign in an out-of-control agency once and for all. What has been done to you, your wife and your children in the name of protecting the children has been done before, but this time one of their own, their so-called finest, has gone off the deep end. Their reign of terror against decent parents like you and your wife and unsuspecting children like yours can now come to an end, if you will let me."

Hesitatingly, "I don't know. I have to think about the children."

Affirmatively, "I know, and the children will be protected every inch of the way. Discretion will be maintained. Nothing will be done without explaining it to you and getting your approval first. No one is going to become a circus act or a media show. I will simply work behind the scenes legally, properly, confidentially. And when I am done, only God will recognize that office." Laughs. "I really shouldn't laugh and I don't want to make you uncomfortable, but if you will let me, one source of evil can finally be controlled. And knowing the type of man you are and how we talk, even as we refer to the good book, I expect you want to see evil's reign come to an end. I am offering you this God-given opportunity. Do you understand?"

"Yes, I do, and yes, I want to see something done to ensure such as Brown can't do to children what has been done to my children. And yes, the agency screwed me over, screwed my children over and clearly screwed my wife over. There has to be a better way to deal with what my wife did than how they treated us."

Very slowly and deliberately, "That is precisely what I am offering. How CAD treats parents and children in the future will change because of what has happened to you, your wife and your children. I can guarantee such change will be comprehensive and exhaustive, not cosmetic, if you let me." Quiet on the line for about ten seconds. "Please, let me do this. There are a lot of children and a lot of parents in CAD limbo, and more will be forthcoming unless you are willing to stop this evil once and for all."

Reluctantly, "Okay, but I must be carefully and completely briefed each step of the way and no legal mumble jumble. I have to understand each action. And I have to approve everything. Nothing can happen without my explicit say-so. Is that clear?"

"Absolutely, and since this is recorded, you will receive a copy of our conversation and a legal affirmation on my part to what you have just requested. For good measure, it will be done in clear, non-legal language. And if you like, you can take it to another lawyer to ensure it is legally binding. Have that lawyer sign off on it before I do my thing."

"Fair enough. I better call my wife."

"Do that, and just make sure she knows I will be in touch with her shortly."

"Goodbye."

"Bye." Phones hang up.

Chapter 8

Melissa Gunnarsen's Notes

Hi Mommy. Hi Daddy. I love you both. You told me to write this down. Okay, Mommy. Okay, Daddy. I love you both. Evil woman says she loves me, she doesn't. She only wants me to play with. I am her toy. Mommy and Daddy love me. They care for me. They help me.

I know Mommy was bad. I know Mommy hit me and hit me and hit me. Mommy was bad, but she is not evil. Ann Brown is evil. Mommy never touches my privates. Mommy never plays with my privates. Mommy never says my privates belong to her. Evil woman said that. Evil woman touched my privates. Evil woman played with my privates. Evil woman yes says my privates belong to her.

Nicole says that is wrong. Woman on TV show says that is wrong. Granny Wanda made Nicole and me watch it. Nobody is to touch my privates. That is wrong. To touch my privates is evil. Ann Brown is evil.

She took my clothes off. She played with my privates. She told me not to tell Mommy and Daddy or I would lose Mommy forever. So I said nothing. I don't want to lose Mommy and Daddy.

Now I have Mommy and Daddy home. We are a family again. We are all together again. I am happy again. I was sad when Mommy was not home. Daddy and Granny Wanda were good to me, but I want my Mommy. I need my Mommy. Mommy, I wanted Mommy home.

Mommy said she would come home soon when she was out of our house. But I want Mommy home now. I wanted Mommy home. Now she is home and I am happy. But what about evil woman Ann Brown? Will evil woman get rid of Mommy and Daddy forever? I am scared of evil woman. I haven't seen her since Nicole and I told Mommy, but she might come back. I don't want her to come back. I love Mommy. I love Daddy. Can Mommy and Daddy keep me safe? Can Mommy and Daddy keep me from Ann Brown? Can Mommy and Daddy keep me from Jolene and the others? Can Mommy and Daddy keep me here? Will Nicole and I have to go away?

I have bad dreams at night. I keep seeing Ann Brown coming for me. I keep seeing Ann Brown on top of me. I keep seeing Ann Brown taking off my clothes. I keep seeing Ann Brown smiling her evil smile at me. I keep seeing Ann Brown playing with my privates. I wake up screaming. I yell in the night. Mommy and Daddy come in and tell me not to be afraid; everything will be okay. I hope so, Mommy and Daddy. I hope so. But Ann Brown is evil and she has had me. She could take me again.

Bad dreams happen every night now. I see Ann Brown every night. I don't even want to take naps any more. Ann Brown is in my naptime. I am scared. I scream. I am afraid. Ann Brown is evil and Ann Brown evil wants me. Ann Brown keeps coming in my dreams, keeps coming, keeps coming, keeps coming. Help me. I don't want Ann Brown. I am scared of Ann Brown.

Mommy, Daddy, keep Ann Brown away. Why did she do that? Why does she do that? Why do I have bad dreams? I am only a little girl. I am told little girls should not go through what I did. That is nice, but I don't feel better. I went through it anyway. And all I see in my dreams is Ann Brown, evil Ann Brown, always Ann Brown. She is coming to get me. She will get me. Mommy, Daddy you can't stop her.

I love you Mommy and Daddy. I do. But I have to protect you. I have to save you. I have to make sure you don't get taken away. Maybe I will have to go to Ann Brown to save you,

Mommy and Daddy. I don't want to, but I have to save you Mommy and Daddy. Maybe if I go to her, you won't be hurt, you won't have to go away. You will still have Nicole.

Evil woman may get me after all. I would do that for you, Mommy and Daddy. But you say that won't happen. You say evil woman can never come near me again. You say evil woman is going to be punished. You say evil woman is going to jail. You say evil woman can never hurt me again. How do you know? How do you know?

And I have to tell what evil woman did to me to certain people. I have to tell a judge and people like Jolene about Ann Brown. I have to be "explicit," the lawyer said, telling everything, not keeping back anything. I have to tell what happened, when it happened, where it happened. I have to tell all the words Ann Brown said to me. I have to be brave. I have to be calm. I have to tell the truth. Why?

She scares me and I don't know I can tell everything. If I have to see her again, I won't say anything. She scares me so. I am only a child. But I want to kill her. I want someone to beat her up. Maybe I will go back to her and I will be long enough with her to find a way to kill her. But I might not live so long. Ann Brown is evil and how long would she let me live? She knows what I think. She heard me call her evil. And she laughs at it. She thinks it is funny. What if she doesn't think it is funny anymore? I am scared of Ann Brown. She gives me bad dreams. She is my bad dream.

Mommy and Daddy love me. They are trying to do the best for me. They want to stop Ann Brown. I don't know if she can be stopped. I wish she could be stopped. Mommy and Daddy say if I talk and tell the truth Ann Brown will be stopped. Mommy and Daddy also say Jolene and people like her won't bother me anymore. They won't bother Mommy and Daddy anymore. We will be a family forever. I will have Mommy and Daddy with me forever.

I want my Mommy. I want my Daddy. They cannot go away. Mommy cannot go away again. I won't let her. I will kill evil woman myself. But Mommy and Daddy say if I talk to people I won't have to kill evil woman. Mommy and Daddy say if I talk other people will help me. Then I won't have bad dreams anymore. Then I can be myself again. Maybe I won't have tantrums anymore. Maybe Mommy won't have to hit me again. Maybe I won't be bad anymore. Mommy and Daddy say it will happen.

All these things will happen. I will be better. Mommy will be better. Mommy and Daddy will be with me. I just have to talk and tell the truth. Don't lie. Don't let evil woman Ann Brown get to me, Mommy said. I want to believe Mommy and Daddy. God, help me to believe Mommy and Daddy. God, I pray to you to help Mommy and Daddy and me and Nicole. God, look down on me and save me from Ann Brown.

God, make me a good girl. God, stop the evil woman. God, help me, so I cannot be afraid. God, help me, so I can say the right words. God, help me, so good people will stop evil woman. God, help me to do what Mommy and Daddy want me to do. God, help me, help me, help me. Amen.

Chapter 9

The Agency's
In-house Interview

As required by state regulations, when a staff member of a governmental agency is accused of misconduct, an in-house interview must be conducted first with the accusers and then with the accused. Such an interview, however, must be conducted by at least three persons who do not know either the accused or the accusers. Often, that means bringing persons in from elsewhere in the state to conduct said interviews. When children are somehow involved, one or two of the interviewers must be board certified in child psychology in order to ascertain whether what the children are saying is true or not.

Because in this case sexual abuse against children is alleged against a social worker in the Children's Affair Division, the representatives must be from Children's Affairs Division and the representatives must be experts in child sexual abuse issues. This is not a legal proceeding, but if the employee refuses to answer, the employee is fired on the spot, and the ability to so fire the employee has been upheld by the courts. By the same token, if the accusers do not consent to the interview or do not answer completely, no legal proceedings can be instituted against the agency or the accused. That procedure too has been upheld by the courts.

Since legal proceedings could ensue as a result of these hearings, the agency recognizes and accepts that the courts have an interest in these hearings. District Justice M. Edward Winthrop of the 15th District at the request of Attorney King McMasters and after proper consultation with Children's Affairs Division has ordered that these interviews be conducted with an official court stenographer present. The court stenographer will record the conversations verbatim as a legal transcript available to all parties including the court following the interview. Children's Affairs Division will pay for the cost of transcribing and distributing the transcripts.

For the sake of the record, the three interviewers are Ralph Winston, M.D., author of *Sexual Abuse of Children: Analyzing and Working with Sexually Abused Children;* and state Coordinator for Child Sexual Abuse Matters for Children's Affairs Division, Evelyn Pasa Miguel, Director of Internal Investigations for Children's Affairs Division; and Linda Zenta, Senior Case Manager of Region 3 for Children's Affairs Division. I, Ralph Winston, wrote the preceding material and the additional notes that follow. I was appointed chair of this interview committee and thereby I moderated the interviews that follow.

Melissa Gunnarsen and Nicole Gunnarsen were brought to us by their parents and their attorney King McMasters. Neither the parents nor the attorney were present in the room during the interview. Melissa came into the room first.

WINSTON: Let the record note that I, Ralph Winston, will ask the first question of Melissa Gunnarsen, who is sitting in front of me. Your name is Melissa Gunnarsen, right?

MELISSA: Yes, sir.

WINSTON: How old are you now?

MELISSA: I just turned nine.

WINSTON: Good for you. Congratulations and happy birthday.

MELISSA: Thank you.

WINSTON: Do you know why you are here today?

MELISSA: Yes, sir.

WINSTON: Okay, please tell me why you are here today.

MELISSA: Because Ann Brown played with my privates.

ZENTA: Before we go any further, Dr. Winston, I feel we need to lay some groundwork here.

WINSTON: Absolutely, go ahead.

ZENTA: Melissa, I have a picture of a little girl I want to show you. Can you tell me what you see?

MELISSA: She has no clothes on.

ZENTA: That is correct. Can you point out where her privates are?

MELISSA: Right there.

WINSTON: Let the record note that Melissa pointed out the genital area of the little girl.

ZENTA: That is correct. Now, Melissa, who is Ann Brown?

MELISSA: An evil woman.

ZENTA: I mean, how do you know her?

MELISSA: Because she played with my privates.

WINSTON: Let me help here. Ann Brown was one of two women who came to see you and your Mommy and your Daddy after you were hit by your Mommy. Is that right?

MELISSA: Yes, sir.

WINSTON: And Ann Brown told you she worked for Children's Affairs Division? Is that right?

MELISSA: Yes, sir.

MIGUEL: Melissa, sometimes when someone from our division wants to talk to you alone, that person takes you somewhere else in the building. Did Ann Brown take you somewhere else?

MELISSA: She took me and Nicole to my bedroom and then Mommy and Daddy's bedroom.

MIGUEL: Did she play with your privates there?

MELISSA: She grabbed me there with my clothes on, but Daddy came in, so she did not have time to play with my privates.

MIGUEL: Do you remember the first time she played with your privates?

MELISSA: Yes, ma'am.

MIGUEL: How soon was it after the first time she met you?

MELISSA: One week.

MIGUEL: Can you tell us exactly how it happened?

MELISSA: Yes, ma'am. She was talking to me and Nicole. And she said, "Sometimes, mommies hit children all over. So I need to see where you were hit. But to do this, I need you, Melissa, to take off all your clothes now and show me all the places your Mommy hit you." I took off my clothes. She asked me where Mommy had hit me and I pointed to my face. She then said, "Nowhere else?"

"No," I said.

She touched my privates and said, "Sometimes mommies hit here or touch here. Did she hit you here or touch you here?"

"No," I said.

She said, "Sometimes we don't want to tell the truth about mommies, even when they do bad things, because we love them. You love your Mommy, don't you?"

"Yes, I do," I said.

She asked me, "Would you lie for your mommy?" I started to cry. I love my Mommy, I do. I love my Mommy. I love my Mommy.

WINSTON: So you could not answer her when she asked you that question?

MELISSA: No, sir.

WINSTON: And what was Ann Brown doing while you cried?

MELISSA: She kept a hand on my privates and she put her other hand around me and hugged me tight.

ZENTA: Wait a minute. Did she have her hand on your privates all this time?

MELISSA: Yes, ma'am.

ZENTA: And she hugged you while you had no clothes on?

MELISSA: Yes, ma'am.

ZENTA: While she was hugging you, did she touch you anywhere else?

MELISSA: She touched me everywhere.

ZENTA: Can you show me on the picture of the doll places she touched you?

MELISSA: Here. Here. Here. Here. Here.

ZENTA: Let the record note that Melissa pointed to her face, her chest, her legs, her back and her buttocks.

MIGUEL: Did she just touch you in those places or did she caress those places?

MELISSA: I don't know what caress means.

MIGUEL: Caress means to move her hands over one place over and over and feel and touch many times the same place. Did she do that?

MELISSA: Yes, ma'am.

MIGUEL: Oh my God.

WINSTON: Yes, this is an ugly picture, but we need to try to keep our emotions under control.

MIGUEL: Easy for you to say, Dr. Winston. I can't and I won't.

ZENTA: We need to get back to this.

WINSTON: We do, but the picture has been made clear to all of us, so we do not need to go into much more detail. I am going to cut this short. Melissa, did your sister Nicole see all this?

MELISSA: Yes, sir.

WINSTON: Great.

MIGUEL: Now, who can't keep his emotions under control?

WINSTON: Point taken. I am sorry, you are right. This is emotional stuff. But Melissa, did she do this to you other times?

MELISSA: Yes, sir.

WINSTON: All of those times with Nicole present?

MELISSA: No, but then sometimes she did this to Nicole too.

ZENTA: Did you see her do this to Nicole too?

MELISSA: Yes, ma'am. Every time I cried after she touched me, she would touch Nicole and she would smile at me.

ZENTA: Can you tell me what the smile was like?

MELISSA: In Sunday School, I saw pictures of Satan smiling. It was like that.

ZENTA: Whew! While she was touching Nicole, did anything else happen between you and her?

MELISSA: Sometimes she would touch me again. Sometimes she would talk to me and tell me I belonged to her now and she could do anything she wanted to me. She always would say, "I love you."

WINSTON: I love you? She said that?

MELISSA: Yes, sir. She would say that every time she touched me.

WINSTON: Justifying her behavior, no doubt, Evelyn and Linda.

ZENTA: That's what it sounds like to me.

MIGUEL: It also means we have a pedophile in our midst.

WINSTON: Great.

MIGUEL: Our work is going to be cut out for us after this.

ZENTA: Tell me about it.

WINSTON: I don't think we need to hear any more from Melissa. Do my colleagues agree we can let her go?

ZENTA: Yes.

MIGUEL: Absolutely.

WINSTON: You can leave, Melissa. Let the record note that Melissa Gunnarsen has left the room. I need to ask my colleagues their impressions before we call in Nicole Gunnarsen. Remember, we are on record here.

MIGUEL: We have a problem, a big problem. That is not a lying child.

ZENTA: The questions I asked and how she answered them leaves me with no doubt in my mind. If Nicole even affirms just a bit of what Melissa said, we are going to have to recommend criminal action against Ann Brown.

WINSTON: Let's not get ahead of ourselves here. Melissa sounds like a credible witness to me, but I do want to hear Nicole, especially before we take any action against Ann Brown. Also, don't forget we will have to hear from Ann Brown too before we can make any recommendations.

ZENTA: I can hardly wait for Ann Brown. But first we have to hear Nicole.

MIGUEL: Call her in.

WINSTON: Let the record note that Nicole Gunnarsen has entered the room. Your name is Nicole Gunnarsen, is that right?

NICOLE: Yes, sir, it is.

WINSTON: How old are you?

NICOLE: I am eleven, but I will be twelve in one month.

WINSTON: I will wish you a happy birthday a month in advance, okay?

NICOLE: Thank you.

WINSTON: Can you tell me why you are here today?

NICOLE: Because your social worker Ann Brown molested Melissa and me, and you are trying to find some way to protect yourselves and her.

MIGUEL: Whew! I know you are angry, Nicole, and you have every right to be angry. But I promise you Ann Brown will go to jail if she molested you. By the way, how do you know the word "molest?"

NICOLE: I heard it used on a TV program I watched that told about what happened to me and other children. It was the word they used on TV, and I looked it up in the dictionary and learned it was the right word.

MIGUEL: That is the right word indeed.

ZANTA: Again, I do need to lay some background here.

WINSTON: Go ahead.

ZANTA: Nicole, what am I holding up?

NICOLE: A picture of a naked girl.

ZANTA: Can you show me where her privates are?

NICOLE: If you mean genitals, down here. If you mean her breasts too, up here.

WINSTON: Let the record note she pointed to the appropriate places on the picture.

ZANTA: Now, did Ann Brown touch you in your private areas?

NICOLE: Yes indeed.

ZANTA: Do you know how many times?

97

NICOLE: Six times.

MIGUEL: How do you know she molested you six times?

NICOLE: Every time Melissa cried, she would grab me, take my clothes off and put her hands hard on my breasts and my genitals. She would look at Melissa the whole time she was molesting me. She never even looked at me, and she said she was doing it to teach Melissa a lesson. I counted the times she did it to me because she made me watch many other times, a lot of times she did it to Melissa. I knew if Melissa cried, my turn would be next. And I prayed Melissa would not cry. But Melissa could only not cry for so long. After a while she had to cry and I could tell she was going to cry, so I counted. I counted. I counted. I counted. I…

MIGUEL: It's okay, Nicole.

NICOLE: No, it's not okay. She did things to Melissa and me she should not have done. Nicole calls her an evil woman, and Ann Brown is an evil woman. And I can't take it, I want to cry now.

WINSTON: Go ahead and cry now. Here's a tissue.

MIGUEL: Let the record note that Nicole is crying uncontrollably. God help her. God help us all.

ZANTA: Can we take a break here?

WINSTON: Yes, let's break for fifteen minutes, we'll go off the record until then.

(a break in the record here until) Okay, fifteen minutes has elapsed, we are back on record. Nicole, do you think you can answer some more questions now?

NICOLE: I'll try.

ZANTA: You said Ann Brown said she was doing it to you to teach Melissa a lesson. Did she ever say what she meant by that?

NICOLE: Sure, she said Melissa belonged to her and Melissa would always belong to her. Touching me was Melissa's punishment for crying, and Melissa knew this. So Melissa would try not to cry so I would not be touched. But Melissa is only a little girl and she could not help crying. Melissa wanted to protect me from Ann Brown, but she couldn't.

MIGUEL: Ann Brown said Melissa belonged to her?

NICOLE: Yes she did, many times.

MIGUEL: Did she ever say why she felt Melissa belonged to her?

NICOLE: Sure, she said Melissa was the love of her life and could never be separated from her.

WINSTON: Did she ever say why Melissa could never be separated from her?

NICOLE: Sure. She said she would see to it that Melissa never went back home again. She would find a way. She had "influence" — that was the word she used. Melissa would belong to her. She said the whole agency would back her. She said everybody knew her and would do for her whatever she wanted. Ann Brown said Melissa better get used to it because she belonged to her now.

MIGUEL: Melissa Gunnarsen belonged to Ann Brown now?

NICOLE: That is what she said, and we believed her.

ZANTA: Why?

NICOLE: She had us. She could do what she wanted with us and even when we saw Mom she would tell us that was the only way we would ever see her. And she told us Dad could do nothing about it. She already had him where she wanted him, so we should see Melissa belonged to Ann Brown now and forever more. That was just the way it was.

WINSTON: The gall of that woman.

MIGUEL: My God.

ZANTA: God has nothing to do with this; Satan maybe.

WINSTON: We are dealing with pure evil in this one.

ZANTA: We have to stop this now.

WINSTON: Okay, but first let's dismiss Nicole Gunnarsen, unless someone has other questions of the child.

ZANTA: No.

MIGUEL: No.

WINSTON: You may leave, Nicole. Let the record note that Nicole Gunnarsen has left the room.

ZANTA: Do we even have to call Ann Brown in after these conversations?

MIGUEL: Yes, we do. We are required by guidelines to do so or else we cannot go any further in this investigation, and we cannot push criminal charges unless she is questioned by us.

ZANTA: I am really looking forward to that.

WINSTON: I know you were being cynical, but Evelyn Pasa Miguel is quite correct. We must interview Ann Brown. So we might as well set a date for doing so and require her presence. I know it will take the court stenographer a few days to provide us with a proper transcript of what has been said so far, and I want time to digest all of this before interviewing Ann Brown. So how about one week from today?

ZANTA: Fine.

MIGUEL: It works for me.

WINSTON: We will see you all in one week. Make sure you read the transcript and be prepared for the interview with Ann Brown. This meeting is over.

The following is the record of the conversation with Ann Brown one week later.

Ann Brown is now present in the room.

WINSTON: Let us introduce ourselves. My name is Dr. Ralph Winston.

MIGUEL: I am Evelyn Pasa Miguel.

ZANTA: And I am Linda Zanta.

BROWN: I am Ann Brown.

WINSTON: As you have been informed, we represent the agency and are here to ask you questions concerning accusations that have been made against you.

BROWN: Which accusations I fully deny.

ZANTA: I have a picture I would like to show you. Would you be so kind as to describe it to me?

BROWN: It is a picture of a girl.

ZANTA: Would you be a little more explicit in your description of this girl?

BROWN: She looks about nine or ten. She has light brown hair. She appears to be Caucasian. Her eyes are a bluish-green.

She looks about normal height and weight and has a normal facial appearance. She is wearing no jewelry that I can ascertain and I don't see any make-up on her. Is that what you want?

ZANTA: How should I address you? Ann? Miss Brown? Ms. Brown? Or something else?

BROWN: Ann is fine.

ZANTA: Okay, Ann, do you notice anything else about this girl?

BROWN: Oh, you mean that she does not have any clothes on and she is the picture of a girl you use to ask those who are sexually abused where they were abused.

ZANTA: Yes, you are aware of this picture and its use. Thank you. I imagine you have used this picture before in your investigations?

BROWN: Of course.

ZANTA: And how do you use it when you approach a child when there is a suspicion of sexual abuse?

BROWN: I ask the child to if they have been touched on their privates and if so, where, or I ask them if anybody took off their clothes and started touching their bodies. I show them the picture and have them point out to me where they have been touched. And if they point to the genitals I know we have a case of sexual abuse.

MIGUEL: What do you do if you learn about sexual abuse after showing the picture?

BROWN: I immediately notify my superiors and call the police. We immediately remove a child from such a situation and have the offending party arrested. It is then up to the person so removed to prove he or she is not a sexual abuser.

MIGUEL: That is very appropriate and clearly follows the regulations.

BROWN: Thank you.

WINSTON: How seriously do you take children when they make such accusations?

BROWN: Very seriously. Of course, I know they can lie but more often than not they are telling the truth. And we have to act as if they are telling the truth.

WINSTON: Quite correct. All within agency guidelines. I commend you on your awareness of agency procedures, protocols and directions. You are very well-informed.

BROWN: Thank you.

WINSTON: Having heard what you have just said, we have two children who have accused you of sexually abusing them. Why should we believe you over them?

BROWN: Because I am innocent of these charges. And to prove that I am innocent, I urge you to ask me what happened, when, where. Use the basic storyline and their accusations to question me, and you will hear a different story from what the children told. After all, parents do manipulate the system for their own purposes as all three of you are quite aware.

WINSTON: We are aware of that fact.

BROWN: So please ask away. I have nothing to hide.

WINSTON: At the first meeting with the children and the mother, did you take the children out of the room where the mother was located?

BROWN: Absolutely, as required by policy guidelines in order to ascertain the truth of whether or not a child-abuse situation had taken place. Keeping the children apart from the mother or the suspected abuser is policy, as you are aware.

WINSTON: We understand that, but we need to know where you took them and what happened as a result.

BROWN: As indicated in the report, I took them both to their room and the master bedroom to appreciate the geography of the situation. I asked them the usual questions and after a number of probes, I was able to ascertain one child had been abused.

ZANTA: Melissa Gunnarsen?

BROWN: Yes.

ZANTA: Melissa Gunnarsen?

BROWN: Yes.

ZANTA: Melissa Gunnarsen?

BROWN: That is the third time you asked me her name and I replied yes both previous times, and I am saying yes again.

ZANTA: Why won't you say her name?

BROWN: Excuse me, I don't understand…

ZANTA: You have said yes three times when I have identified her name, but you have not said her name yourself. Why?

BROWN: I just respond to the questions and that question seemed to me to be a simple yes or no question, so I responded accordingly.

ZANTA: Please say the name of the child who was abused by her mother.

BROWN: Huh? Oh, okay, her name as indicated in the record is Melissa Gunnarsen.

ZANTA: Just for the record, state only her name.

BROWN: Hmmm. Okay, Melissa Gunnarsen.

ZANTA: And hereafter when the child is referred to, I expect you to give her name. Is that understood?

BROWN: Yes.

MIGUEL: Did you physically touch her at this time?

BROWN: Well, I did embrace her at one time because I felt maternal sorrow for the child, and that I know is not against the rules. Surely you don't think that was somehow me molesting her.

MIGUEL: Embracing a child after being abused is not molesting a child, of course. Just out of curiosity, why did you use the word "molesting?"

BROWN: Isn't that what I am accused of doing?

MIGUEL: Sexual abuse, as you are aware, includes any number of possibilities including molesting. We are trying to determine whether you were sexually abusing one or both of these children in any form or fashion, so…

BROWN: Whatever form I am supposed to have done, I deny it.

ZANTA: Well, let's get back to the story. Did you on that first night in any form or fashion sexually abuse Melissa Gunnarsen?

BROWN: No.

ZANTA: No what?

BROWN: I did not molest her.

ZANTA: I asked you before to name her when she was referred to. Did you sexually abuse Melissa Gunnarsen?

BROWN: I did not sexually abuse Melissa Gunnarsen, okay?

WINSTON: There are certain ground rules for how we conduct this, Ann, and we do expect you to honor them. Now Linda Zanta specifically asked you to state the name of the child, Melissa Gunnarsen, every time she is referred to. Please do so from this point on. Do you understand?

BROWN: Yes, sir, I do.

WINSTON: You did not molest Melissa Gunnarsen then?

BROWN: I did not molest Melissa Gunnarsen then.

WINSTON: Over the course of the various times you met with Melissa Gunnarsen and her sister Nicole Gunnarsen, did you touch either of them in their genitals?

BROWN: I did not molest, touch, sexually abuse, whatever, Melissa Gunnarsen or Nicole Gunnarsen.

WINSTON: Did you have Melissa Gunnarsen take her clothes off during any of the interviews in order to ascertain whether or not she had been beaten around her backside or her privates?

BROWN: Of course, that is also agency policy as you well know. How else can one ascertain how severely she had been beaten unless one inspects modestly the entire child's body?

WINSTON: This is Melissa Gunnarsen we are talking about, the child whom you are supposed to name each time you mention anything about her?

BROWN: I am sorry, I am just not used to saying a child's name. But yes, Melissa Gunnarsen is the child and she was asked to take her clothes off by me, Ann Brown, in order to ascertain whether she had been beaten where her clothes would hide marks.

MIGUEL: Did Jolene Wilcox ever have Melissa Gunnarsen or Nicole Gunnarsen take their clothes off in her presence?

BROWN: No. Melissa and Nicole only took off their clothes in my presence.

MIGUEL: Why not?

BROWN: It was not necessary. No bruises were located where clothes would hide them.

MIGUEL: Shouldn't that have been confirmed by Jolene Wilcox?

BROWN: I did not see the necessity of doing so. After all, why expose the girls, Melissa and Nicole, to more embarrassment than they already endured?

MIGUEL: Indeed. Did you have Melissa Gunnarsen and Nicole Gunnarsen take off their clothes more than once?

BROWN: I only had Melissa and Nicole do that once.

ZANTA: How did you inspect Melissa Gunnarsen when she was naked?

BROWN: I looked over her body for bruises. I mean, I looked over Melissa Gunnarsen when she was unclothed for bruises.

ZANTA: Did you touch Melissa Gunnarsen when she was naked?

BROWN: Of course not, why should I touch Melissa Gunnarsen?

MIGUEL: Actually, certain bruises cannot be determined by the eye alone and thus require a slight touch to see if the child, here Melissa Gunnarsen, evinced pain. And considering that you and Jolene had Melissa in your custody and care, the two of you could have touched gently to see if she responded in pain. It would be another reason to have Jolene Wilcox inspect Melissa as well.

BROWN: I did not think about that, as I guess I was just thinking about the child's, er, Melissa Gunnarsen's welfare.

WINSTON: That is, of course, departmental policy, in order to ascertain the truth and to prevent situations like what we are facing today. Two witnesses are better than one, and two people ensure that one does not cross the bounds. And for a person so attuned to agency policy, this is disappointing.

BROWN: I guess I was not thinking. I really did not expect anything like this.

WINSTON: No one does. Now tell me your personal impressions of Melissa Gunnarsen.

BROWN: Melissa Gunnarsen is a sweet, adorable young child who is unfortunate to have a mother beat her and thus it is my duty to help her.

ZANTA: Why do you call Melissa Gunnarsen sweet and adorable?

BROWN: Why if you met her you would know she is very pretty and she has a wonderful disposition! It is a shame what happened to her, uh, Melissa Gunnarsen, by her abusive mother.

ZANTA: Yes it is. And you wanted to make sure Angela Gunnarsen did not do it again, is that right?

BROWN: Absolutely.

ZANTA: Were you aware that Melissa Gunnarsen is diagnosed hyperactive?

BROWN: I was told that.

ZANTA: How did you respond to that?

BROWN: I was skeptical.

ZANTA: Did the agency investigate this claim?

BROWN: It did.

ZANTA: And what did it find?

BROWN: She was diagnosed hyperactive and nothing psychologically had been effective in controlling her extreme mood swings.

WINSTON: Yet when I asked you for your personal impressions of Melissa Gunnarsen, you said she was sweet and adorable. In light of the agency investigation, why?

BROWN: She is sweet and adorable. Even when she goes off, she does not mean it. Melissa Gunnarsen is sweet and adorable despite her past history.

MIGUEL: Is it true that Melissa has attacked you?

BROWN: Once, but that was her anger at being separated from her mother.

MIGUEL: Is it also true that Melissa Gunnarsen calls you the evil woman?

BROWN: I am sure she doesn't mean anything by it; I'm just the intermediary between her and her mother. So naturally in good psychological manner, she is projecting her anger with her mother at me. I am just the natural target.

MIGUEL: You are just the natural target? How did that come about? I really don't understand that statement.

BROWN: Well, she is with me a lot and since she can't focus in on her mother, she focuses her anger in on me. Melissa Gunnarsen, that is, I know I keep forgetting to say her name.

WINSTON: And despite all of these facts, you still find her sweet and adorable?

BROWN: Of course, she is a wonderful child, is Melissa Gunnarsen, and she deserves better.

WINSTON: Could you explain "she deserves better"?

BROWN: She definitely did not deserve being beaten. She definitely deserved a mother who understood her and cared for her and would not resort to violence. She needed a mother who loved her and truly appreciated her. And she could use a father who knew how to intervene and prevent such abuse from happening. So in short she deserved to be loved.

WINSTON: By you?

BROWN: I really don't understand the question.

MIGUEL: Dr. Winston has asked a very straightforward question. In light of what happened to Melissa Gunnarsen by her mother Angela Gunnarsen and the fact her father Andrew Gunnarsen was unaware and did not intervene, does Melissa deserve to be loved by you?

BROWN: I love all the children I have to deal with. It is the only way to help them after they have been abused.

MIGUEL: Yes, but did Melissa Gunnarsen deserve to be loved by you?

BROWN: Of course, Melissa Gunnarsen deserved to be loved by me. I deserved to love her. She had to appreciate love to be loved again by her mother, her father and anyone she would later fall in love with.

MIGUEL: Do you love Melissa Gunnarsen?

BROWN: I love all the children I have to deal with. As I said...

MIGUEL: Yes, I know what you said, but do you love Melissa Gunnarsen?

BROWN: As I said…

WINSTON: We know what you said and that we understand. But do you love Melissa Gunnarsen?

BROWN: Of course, she is a sweet, adorable child. She deserves better than what she has received in her life so far.

WINSTON: Yes. And you deny touching, molesting, caressing or otherwise sexually abusing Melissa Gunnarsen?

BROWN: Absolutely.

WINSTON: And you deny touching, molesting, caressing or otherwise sexually abusing Nicole Gunnarsen?

BROWN: Absolutely.

WINSTON: I think that will be enough questioning of you, unless my colleagues have some further questions?

ZANTA: I have none.

MIGUEL: Neither do I.

WINSTON: Ann Brown, you are dismissed. Let the record note Ann Brown has left the room.

ZANTA: She is guilty as hell.

MIGUEL: I might not use that same phrase, but Ann Brown did sexually abuse Melissa Gunnarsen. There is no doubt about that in my mind.

WINSTON: Of course, she confessed to violating departmental policy about dealing with children when nudity is called for. That would automatically get her a full-scale departmental reprimand and would guarantee she goes nowhere else in the agency.

ZANTA: You are not stopping with just that, are you Dr. Winston?

WINSTON: Oh no. You misunderstood me. I am pointing out an obvious violation and using that as a springboard for what comes hereafter. She could not get beyond seeing Melissa Gunnarsen as a sweet, adorable child, and that is clearly un-objective and showing feeling for the child.

MIGUEL: She did declare her love for Melissa Gunnarsen.

ZANTA: And how many times did she struggle even to say "Melissa Gunnarsen!"

WINSTON: And that was despite my constant insistence she do so. There are so many problems with that. Sexual abusers often do not like the given name as that ties the victim to a family the sexual abuser does not recognize. Sometimes the name becomes too "holy" as it were to be said by the abuser and can only be said in part or in whole while the abuser is in the act of abusing the victim.

MIGUEL: As director of Internal Investigations for Children's Affairs Division, I must recommend criminal actions be instituted against Ann Brown.

ZANTA: I fully agree and she must be immediately suspended without pay.

MIGUEL: Quite correct. And you, Dr. Winston?

WINSTON: I unequivocally make this unanimous, and I will be glad to write up the rationale if you like and submit it to you for your corrections, additions and ultimately approval.

MIGUEL: That works for me.

ZANTA: Amen. Count me in.

Chapter 10

The Newspaper Reports

(Report 1)

Children's Affairs Division social worker Ann Brown was arrested in her office on charges of sexually molesting two young girls. She had no comment when reporters asked her about the charges. However, her attorney later issued a statement declaring that "she would plead not guilty and fight these unjustified charges." The attorney also asked the public to remember "Ann Brown is only accused of these crimes, and thus is innocent until proven guilty."

The prosecutor's office has confirmed that the two children were under her supervision. Children's Affairs Division among its other responsibilities handles all cases of child abuse. Ann Brown was overseeing the two children because their mother had abused one of the two children. The children still lived with their father, but the division oversees them while the case is still considered active.

The mother was on the verge of being reunited with her children and going home to her husband when these accusations arose. An independent panel of the division investigated first and recommended criminal actions be brought against Ann Brown.

Division staff present at the arrest were stunned. "I can't believe this," said one staffer who wished not to be named.

Other staffers voiced similar sentiments. A collective moan was heard as Ann Brown was led out in handcuffs.

Jolene Wilcox, who worked with Ann Brown on the case, insisted nothing happened. "Ann Brown is the consummate professional. These are lies. I would have known if something like these charges had actually happened."

Immediately after she made this comment to reporters, she was served a subpoena by the prosecutor's office. Ms. Wilcox was so shocked by the subpoena she fled into her office and refused to speak further. The prosecutor's office confirmed that Ms. Wilcox will be required to testify at the trial of Ann Brown.

Clients present at the division office were clearly shaken and scared. One client was heard in the distance asking, "How can I trust my children to these people?" Another client was heard giving a shrill whistle.

The office devolved into chaos as staff and clients started shouting at each other. People were pounding desks. Some object unidentified was seen thrown across the room. At that moment, extra police came in and quickly restored order. No one was arrested and no further charges will be laid against anyone in the office.

Originally, the arrest was to be done discretely and out of the public eye, but a leak to the press made that impossible. The prosecutor's office agreed to go public with both the arrest and trial provided the press did not report on the case until the arrest. The press, in turn, would be present at the arrest. Also, neither the children nor the family could ever be identified. The press agreed to these terms.

The prosecutor released a statement from the family after the arrest. The family noted, "We are deeply unhappy with how the arrest has been handled. We urge the media to remember children's lives are at stake here. We understand this is a major story, but we also urge responsibility. Please do not make this into a media circus. As to the charges themselves, we are relieved and grateful. Now we can only hope justice will be done, and Ann Brown will be sent to the prison she so rightfully deserves. God, help us all."

(Report 3)

Accused child molester Ann Brown was brought in handcuffs and prison clothing into the courtroom of District Justice M. Edward Winthrop. Her attorney was present. She was asked how she would plea. Her attorney in a strong voice said, "Innocent, your honor." Standing by her attorney, Ann Brown appeared defiant, even angry. She was overheard speaking loudly to her attorney, "Get me out of here now."

The justice ignored her outbreak and turned to the prosecutor and asked, "What are you proposing for bail?"

"No bail, your honor."

The judge was stunned by this reply, but he quickly composed himself. Ann Brown's attorney started to speak, but the justice told him to be quiet; he would get his turn momentarily.

"Why are you saying no bail?"

"We have a sexual predator here, your honor. We can show this is not the first time she has done this. Letting her loose on the public is a recipe for disaster and more children being attacked. No bail, your honor."

"Counselor?" he turned to the defense attorney.

"That is hearsay, your honor. There have never been any charges for any crime filed against my client. She is as clean as a whistle. Look at what she is being accused of. How do you think she is going to do these so-called actions when everyone is going to be watching her from now on? Further, she denies these actions vehemently. They are lies, your honor. And for good measure, her very livelihood depends on her being in town. Case law is clearly on the side of allowing bail in this case."

"Except when she is a danger to the community," interjected the prosecutor.

"She has not been charged with anything previously, has she?"

"No, your honor."

"Do you have other charges pending?"

"No, your honor."

"Has she been declared a sexual predator?"

"No, your honor."

"I appreciate your concern, but my hands are tied. I have to grant bail. I will require she not be anywhere near children nor be allowed back to work in her office. She will be monitored electronically to ensure she does not go to places children are. Two hundred thousand dollars bail."

"Your honor, that is excessive."

"No, it is not. Be thankful I did not say a million. I am granting bail, but I need to keep aware of the prosecutor's concerns."

The bail money was presented to the court immediately upon the conclusion of the hearing. Ann Brown was released from custody, and she smiled. Asked her comments, she declined. She is now staying at an undisclosed location, but she is being electronically monitored.

(Report 6)

Attorney King McMasters has filed a civil suit on behalf of the family of the two girls against both the Children's Affairs Division and Ann Brown. The family to be unnamed in the lawsuit is seeking unspecified damages. The division had no comment, citing the pending legal action. Ann Brown's attorney once again denied the accusations and insisted her client would fight the charges aggressively.

Attorney McMasters, when contacted by this reporter, was very open. "You ain't seen anything yet," he began. "I have already been approached by parents of other girls who were molested by Ann Brown. And these were all children under her supervision as a social worker for the Children's Affairs Division. What type of agency is being run there? I guarantee there will be numerous lawsuits against the agency. Of course, the courts could consolidate the cases. The division is going to pay big league for its incompetence. How could it not know what was going on with its own staff? The division is diabolic."

We cannot quote the remainder of Attorney McMaster's comments, as they were a series of profanities aimed at the division.

(Report 7)

True to his word, Attorney King McMasters has filed three new lawsuits against the Children's Affairs Division and Ann Brown. They also are unnamed plaintiffs seeking unspecified damages. Attorney McMaster's office has acknowledged being "flooded by accusations against Ann Brown and the division. We expect to take the time needed to investigate all such allegations and to file the legal work needed thereafter."

The division still refuses to respond to the accusations. However, sources within the division indicate there is much dissension in the agency. A number of representatives in the division are calling for contact to be made with Attorney McMasters and to find some way to settle these cases immediately "before they get out of hand, and the division's authority is totally undermined." Others reject this and want to fight to the end.

It is expected that the division will seek a gag order, apparently to prevent Attorney McMasters from commenting further. Also, the division will insist that all evidence be sealed, thus preventing it from becoming public knowledge at least until the trial is over.

Ann Brown has refused any further comment. Her attorney insists she will no longer respond to "these ongoing, unjustified accusations, which are at best gossip, at worst copycat moneymaking schemes."

Attorney McMasters, upon hearing what the division was planning to do, replied, "I will not be silenced. I speak for people who have been abused by the agency, and we will no longer allow the agency to sweep its problems under the carpet. Too long this agency has gotten out of control. It has lost its moral compass. It is now a bureaucratic nightmare imprisoning people in a maze from which there is no awakening to escape."

Attorney McMasters called on the press to join in his fight to keep the battle public. "If I am silenced, you are silenced too, and the public is not allowed to know the truth."

Based on the possibility of a gag order, Media Network, of which this paper is a part, has gone on record as indicating it will fight such an order. Other press and media have also agreed to join in fighting such a gag order.

(Report 9)

District Justice M. Edward Winthrop rejected a gag order in the case of Ann Brown. He was quite emphatic. "Such an order would be detrimental to the public's right to know." He dismissed as "conjecture" the argument that without a gag order the client would not get a fair trial. He insisted that the Children's Affairs Division would have to stand up for itself and could not hide behind any screen of secrecy just because it was getting bad publicity.

The Honorable Justice Winthrop went further and seriously suggested to the division that "it would be to your benefit to settle these cases while they still can be contained." Representatives of the Children's Affairs Division were seen to scowl at this suggestion. Nonetheless, sources within the agency have made it clear that discussions have now begun with the office of Attorney King McMasters.

An order to suppress the evidence until the trial was granted. However, the justice indicated he would allow the evidence to be made public once the trial began. He went even further and declared that "in light of the publicity surrounding this case, I will entertain a motion to allow the hearing to be televised. Of course, certain restrictions will be put in place, primarily to protect the children, but I am inclined to allow such a motion."

Immediately, television representatives filed such a motion. Apparently, they had been tipped off the justice would allow it. They will cooperate, doing a joint feed by one TV representative.

(Report 10)

In a sudden and unexpected development, Children's Affairs Division and Attorney King McMasters have announced a joint settlement of all pending and future cases involving sexual abuse of children by social worker Ann Brown. While details have not been fully released, apparently a fund of money will be set up under the supervision of Attorney King McMasters to be distributed to alleged victims of Ann Brown. The money is unspecified but may be added to depending on how many additional cases surface.

The division insists there is no acceptance of wrongdoing by the agency. Rather, the settlement is intended to put "this ugly incident behind us, and help the alleged victims get on with their lives." The division insists "we are here to protect children, and this action is intended to make sure the children get the protection they need."

Attorney McMasters welcomed the settlement and promised that all children who were ever abused by Ann Brown will be fairly compensated. He smiled when he said this, and added, "You can draw your own conclusions from this settlement." Representatives of the division were noticeably not pleased when the attorney added this line, but said nothing.

Attempts to reach Ann Brown or her attorney for comment were unsuccessful. However, they have indicated previously they will no longer respond in the media to anything said about this case. They feel the case needs to be tried in court, not the media.

Chapter 11

The Deputy's Report

Children react to me in only two ways. Either they find me cool and want to be around me all the time or they are scared out of their bejammers and stay away from me as if I had the plague. I know it has to be the way I am dressed for court. I have a full-dress blue police uniform on with a broad-rimmed hat, heavy black belt and boots that would make the military proud. And of course, I have that gun hanging by my right side, very obvious, very commanding and very accessible.

Like I said, the kids find it cool or scary. Those who find it cool want a family member or relative to take a picture of them with me, so they can show it to all their friends and fellow students in school. It goes over big and has led me to be invited numerous times to schools to speak about my job. The only requirement for my attendance is I have to be fully dressed up, including the gun. Yes, they always say include the gun and talk about it as part of the uniform and the job.

Those who find my dress scary are like kids who hate to get shots. The only way you will get them near you is to chase them, grab them, hold on to them and not let go. That, of course, only does the child and me so much, but in extreme situations where the court requires it, I have done so. The judge presiding over such a case has even apologized to me for forcing that upon me, but unfortunately that is necessary in such circumstances.

Some kids afraid of me I have found ways to break down the fear, especially if the case requires I be close enough to the child to ensure the child's safety. Oh, Melissa Gunnarsen was definitely scared of me. What am I saying? She was positively flipped out, zonked out, went ballistic at seeing me for the first time. I had never seen anything like it. She screamed, "Mommy, Daddy, save me. This man is going to kill me."

She threw herself onto Mr. Gunnarsen and then half-dragged him to his wife, her mother, and held on for dear life. Her body shook as if she were having a seizure. She screamed incoherently for minutes. And this was in the antechamber to the courtroom. Every lawyer was looking at me. The bailiff was looking at me. People waiting to have their cases heard were looking at me. And for good measure after this went on for a while, out comes the District Justice M. Edward Winthrop himself.

The good judge even had his black robe on. *Great*, I thought, *now I'm in trouble. He must be getting ready to hear a case, and I have this howling banshee out here disrupting his courtroom. Don't I know my job? I am supposed to keep order, and here I am causing disorder.*

"Your honor, I..." began.

But he interrupted me immediately, "Don't panic, Charlie." He always called me by my nickname. He was a good judge, a decent judge, and he always treated me well. He was not the type to blame or get hypercritical or even nasty with those under his authority. I had forgotten that in the moment of listening to Melissa Gunnarsen's ear-piercing screams.

Instead, the honorable District Justice M. Edward Winthrop, he of the white hair, those deep blue eyes that look so paternal and a modest height (not a tall man, but not a small man either), walked over to Melissa and smiled. "You must be Melissa Gunnarsen. My name is Edward Winthrop, Ed if you like. I have a letter I use before my name, M. Do you know why I have an M before my name?" Melissa stopped screaming as he spoke to her and as he asked her the question, she shook her head. "Well," said the District

Justice, "it is because my parents gave me a first name I don't like — yuk, you know what yuk is?"

Melissa shook her head yes, and stuck out her tongue to show him. "That's it, that's yuk all right. You know it. So I have a first name that is yuk."

"What is it?" Melissa asked as only a child can.

"Melissa, don't ask that question of the judge," said her mother. "That is not very polite."

"Oh, that is okay," the district justice replied. "I really don't mind, but Melissa as soon as I tell you, you have to stick out your tongue for me. Will you do that, promise?"

"I will," she replied.

"Good girl. It is Magatz, and yes that is pronounced like maggots. You know what maggots are?"

"Yuk," she replied, and that tongue came out on cue.

I didn't even know that was his first name, and I have been chief deputy in his court for ten years now. Most of the lawyers around him, I could see did not know it either. No one had ever dared ask. Maybe a few knew, some who had lived in the area all their lives, since he did grow up nearby. I do understand he had a bad childhood and struggled through school and had to put up with bullying and worse. I now understand why. I also know why he goes by his middle name.

"Why," continued Melissa, "would your parents name you that?"

Ah yes, children. They ask all the tactless questions everyone would love to have answered, but we don't ask those questions because we are not tactless. Maybe at times we need to ask those tactless questions. It would help explain a lot. It surely did with District Justice Winthrop.

"Sadly," came the answer, "it is an old family name that my mother wanted to make sure remained in the family. And my father chose not to fight her over it because she insisted I be named that. You might guess that kids were not nice to me, and my mother over the years came to feel sorry about naming me that. So when I told her I would only go by my middle name, she did not argue with me or anything. She was proud of me for all I have done, and she said I could call myself anything I wanted."

"Wow," replied Melissa, obviously impressed.

"Now I know you are afraid of my friend Charlie O'Shea over here, that big burly cop. He is bigger than me, and he looks so scary in that outfit he has on. You know he has to put that on, just like I have to wear this big black robe. It is part of my job. It is part of his job. He does not mean to scare you. Charlie and I are great friends, right Charlie?"

"Yes, your honor."

"Charlie?" he looked at me impatiently.

"Yes, Ed." After all these years and all his imprecations to call him Ed, I am of the old school that a person in his position is to be called by his title or some official line of respect. But in this situation, I had to force myself for the sake of Melissa Gunnarsen. She and I would be spending time together in this case, and I had to make that possible, even if it meant calling the right honorable district justice by his nickname.

King McMasters, the family's attorney and a guy I did know by first name, having quaffed a few beers at the local watering hole with him over the years, laughed. He knew me too well and he knew the judge too well and he knew how I reacted to the judge and he just could not stop laughing. Once he began, Ed (hey, I can write it once in a while, I guess) laughed too. And then I began to laugh. Mr. and Mrs. Gunnarsen started to laugh and then Melissa started laughing.

The next thing I knew, Melissa had wiggled her way loose from her parents and came over to me, nervously I could tell, but she did come over to me. "Could you hold me?" she asked me, "and maybe I won't be scared."

This kid was remarkable. I never had a kid anywhere face her fear of me by asking me to hold her. "Of course, come here." I picked her up and she with lips that could not decide whether to smile or frown looked intently at me.

"You are nice, but you are scary."

"I know. But maybe if I go over what all I have on, you might not be so scared of me. What do you think?"

"Okay."

"See, let's start at the top. I have to wear this special police hat because it tells everybody I am a policeman. I can't take it off until I go into the courtroom and the district justice comes in. He is the only person other than my wife who can see me taking my hat off." She laughed when I said my wife.

"Ed doesn't look like your wife, I bet."

"I hope not," came the justice's reply, and everyone was laughing again.

"You see all these badges on me? That tells me and everyone else who I am. You see I have to be reminded of who I am and once I put these on, I say, oh yeah, I am a policeman."

"Oh, you are just kidding me," she said. "You know who you are."

"Sure I do, but not everyone else does. So I wear all this stuff just to let people know who I am and I look good because I want people to feel good about having me as a policeman."

"Okay," she smiled. "But what about those big boots and that, that…" she pointed to the gun. I knew it would come to that eventually.

"The boots I wear because they protect my feet in all kinds of weather and when I have to walk in the mud, the snow, the water. I am sure you like to play in mud and snow and water, and if you had these boots on, your Mom and Dad would not have to yell at you when you got messy."

She turned right to her father and said, "You have to buy me a pair of boots too, okay?"

Her father smiled and said, "You know I will, as soon as all of this is over."

She became serious, before turning her face to me again, "The gun?" She said the word and I knew I had to answer her.

"There are bad people around and sometimes this is the only way to stop them from being bad."

"The only way?" she was fascinated.

"Only in really bad situations when they are trying to hurt other people and they won't stop any other way."

"Can I see it?"

I looked at the judge and I could see he was leaving this up to my best judgment. I looked at her father. I really did not want to do this if the family objected. But her father said, "It might help. Besides, you two are going to be spending a lot of time together." Yes, I would be the one escorting the child in by herself, apart from her parents. Once the trial started, she would be kept separate from her parents, the lawyers, anybody in the court or around the court, except for me. I would be with her constantly, and I knew it. So I had to at least try to keep her trust. It would make the courtroom scene quieter and ensure justice was done.

The kid was going to have to deal with a lot during the courtroom proceedings, and she didn't need me to make things worse. So I pulled the gun out of the holster, but I made sure the safety was still on before I let her examine it. She didn't take it from me or anything. I held on to it the whole time, but I let her see it and I let her touch it.

She was impressed. I could see that. She kept looking at the gun and then she would look at me. She went back and forth between the gun and me so many times and so rapidly that I quickly lost count. I still don't know what to make of that. Trying to describe the motion, I would use the word hypnotic. Following her motion would be like following one of those hypnosis machines that just go back and forth, and you soon find yourself mesmerized by the motion. I had to look away myself because the motion was definitely forcing me into some sort of trance, and I realized it immediately.

Her parents were intently watching her and I could see they were falling into the trance as well. "Mr. Gunnarsen, do you think she has seen enough?" I interjected immediately to break the spell.

The reaction was immediate. Mr. and Mrs. Gunnarsen looked directly at me and Mrs. Gunnarsen replied, "Absolutely. Melissa, come here."

Melissa jumped out of my arms like my cat at home does when it is tired of me and landed right beside her parents. She was agile, even gymnastic that one. Oh and she was fast!

Between her mother's call and her landing maybe took a few seconds. I will have to keep an eye on that one when we go into trial. Who knows where she will go or what she will do if I am not watching her every move! I better be prepared for anything she does. Now that I know she is this way, you can believe I was ready for her.

Having written that last line though I was amazed how quiet, even compliant, she was as I escorted her into court. She was gentle, meek, a little lamb. And she impressed everyone. Having seen that cat-like side of her and those hypnotic motions, I expected the worst. Instead, I had a child who was a delight. It did not add up, but who am I to argue? This was the way I hoped she would be and the way she really needed to be. And she was.

Huh, maybe I so impressed her; she was exactly what she was supposed to be. Right! Okay, that is the cop cynic coming out in me, after dealing with people all these years. You can only trust people so far. They are bound to sin and sin again, and their sins come out no matter what acts they put on elsewise. They can only fool you so far. That is my cop training. Nonetheless, she was ideal. She was exactly what a good little child should be.

"It's time to go in," I would say to her.

"Yes, sir," she would always reply to me. She would stop whatever she was doing, take my hand and walk with me graciously into the courtroom. She would smile, look pretty and be a cute little doll going as to a child's tea party. She would look for her parents, see them and shake her little head up and down, even once threw kisses to them. Her father laughed and the judge had to reprimand him.

"I know she is your daughter and she is being cute, but you cannot react like that in this courtroom, or I will have to remove you. Is that understood?"

"Yes, your honor."

I am not a lawyer, so I don't fully understand court hearings, even after all these years. I can't serve on juries — the state won't let me. I am just there to ensure calm and to make sure one little child is present in the courtroom when it is her time to say her piece. I could feel the tension in the air. And I could see the prosecutor was none too happy. That mood was typical of court cases anyway, the ones I dealt with. But it seemed a bit worse than usual. Who am I to say?

I just have to lead the child back in again. "Come on, Melissa. It is time to go in again."

"Yes, sir."

Chapter 12

Portions of the TV Coverage

"We are at the trial of Ann Brown, social worker for Children's Affairs Division, accused of sexually molesting two children who were under her supervision. One of the children had been beaten by her mother, which led to the intervention of the division and Ann Brown's becoming involved in the first place. Due to the publicity surrounding this case, the court has provided us with limited access.

"We cannot tell you the names of the children, or show them to you in any way that would give away their identity. When certain witnesses testify, we will be required to cover their faces and occasionally change their voices. The court will tell us when we have to do so. We have also hired the services of Attorney King McMasters. He is the attorney for the parents of the two children, and as such his knowledge of this case will be significant. The parents have approved this arrangement, as has the court. His comments, of course, cannot compromise his attorney-client privilege.

"Let me introduce Attorney McMasters. Welcome to our program, Mr. McMasters."

"Thank you. I am glad to be here."

"What must the prosecution show to convince the jury that Ann Brown did sexually molest the two children?"

"The testimony of the children will be important, of course, but also testimony from others, including adults, who can point out a pattern of problematic behavior."

"This would suggest the defense will have to show that testimony is at best suspect if not wrong."

"As you know, I have a bias in this case, but you are exactly right. If the defense can chop up the testimony of the various witnesses, especially the children, the jury would not be convinced beyond a reasonable doubt."

"Doesn't that also include a risk to the defense? I mean, who wants to be seen as attacking children, or being mean to children in such a stressful situation? It might backfire."

"Precisely. Any attorney questioning children has to handle the children with kids' gloves, meaning very carefully. A jury that sees an adult badgering a child will not support the person doing so, but instead will be sympathetic to the child."

"Thank you, Attorney McMasters. Let us now go inside the courtroom. You are looking at the judge's desk and here comes District Judge M. Edward Winthrop. Let's listen in."

"All rise."

"The people are rising."

"You may be seated."

"In the matter of the People versus Ann Brown, we will hear opening statements. The District Attorney will speak first."

"Thank you, your honor. Members of the jury, I bow to you as you see me doing so. It is your responsibility to deal with an important matter in this trial, children being sexually molested. We intend to prove beyond a shadow of a doubt that the defendant Ann Brown is a sexual predator of children, and two children specifically. When you have heard the evidence, I know you will convict Ann Brown and take away her freedom. And that is why I bowed to you before and I do so again. These children are in your hands, your thoughts, your deliberations. In other words, they need you to do justice and to prevent Ann Brown from continuing her sexual abuse of children. Experts will be presented, including some from the very agency in which Ann Brown works, to show that Ann Brown is the sexual molester of children she is hereby accused of being. I bow to you yet again because you will make the determination that will free the children from this predator and deliver an honorable agency from a criminal. You will hear the children speak. You will hear others who can tell you these children are honest. You will hear from adults who can set a pattern that clearly shows Ann Brown was molesting these children. Evidence will show that Ann Brown did these heinous acts. The facts will speak for themselves. So yes, I bow to you again because I know you will hear and see everything presented in this court and then you will return a verdict of guilty against Ann Brown. Justice will be served because you are in the seats of justice, and you will act for the children's sake."

"Before we go back in and hear the defense attorney's opening statement, Attorney McMasters, do you have any comment?"

"A little too flowery for me. All those bows, give me a break. I just hope the jury doesn't get turned off by that stuff and wonder what type of person he is and what type of case he is going to present."

"Thank you, Attorney McMasters. The defense attorney is rising and about to speak. Let's rejoin the case."

"Your honor and members of the jury, I just want you to hear one word: UNBELIEVABLE! Yep, that is what I said. UNBELIEVABLE! You are about to hear a case that is unbelievable from start to finish. The evidence is shoddy, circumstantial at best. At worst, it is an outright disgrace and requires a science-fiction imagination to make my client look guilty of these ugly crimes. But the prosecution hopes you cannot think rationally but that you think as if your mind were in na-na land. I know better than that. When you hear this flimsy case, you will be shaking your heads and wondering what in the world it is even doing in a courtroom. I know you are going to pay close attention to the witnesses, especially the children. My client has worked with children for years, and we will show these children have some special problems that need to be considered. Worse, you will find out that these children have been pushed into these false accusations by people who should have known better, but they had their own agenda. The parents got rid of the Children's Affairs Division by these accusations. You will hear the whole sordid history of this case, including the key fact that the mother of these children had abused one of them. When her children were taken away from her, she has been conspiring to get them back any way she can, including by concocting this unbelievable story. The sad irony of this case is that she was close to regaining her children, but she had to come up with this unbelievable accusation and influence the children. After you hear the truth, you will wonder why she has the children back. She deceived everyone, including her unfortunate husband, who naturally loves his wife and is willing to believe her because of his blind love. The so-called experts, take with a real grain of salt. Experts can say anything. Hey, we will have experts say exactly the opposite to their experts, and you will start to doubt this whole false concoction. You will see that expert testimony goes only so far. I know that after you hear this case, including my questioning of their witnesses, you will have the doubt needed to find my client innocent. I am willing to go further. Not only will you doubt their case, you will know in your hearts and your minds that this case is a piece of trash and deserves to be treated as the trash it is. You will find my client innocent and you will be proud of your honest verdict."

"Attorney McMasters, your take on the opening statement by the defense attorney."

"I hope the prosecutor is ready for this case. The defense attorney definitely is, if even half of what he is saying he will do in the courtroom is shown."

"We are now a week into this case, and while I am not a lawyer, I am a reporter and I am hearing murmurings from many observers. And they are all murmuring about the prosecutor's handling of the case. What I see and everybody else seems to see is that the prosecutor is presenting the case badly. But let's get a professional opinion — Attorney McMasters?"

"You are exactly right. I don't know what the prosecutor is doing. The case is not being presented sequentially. It is a piece here and a piece there. If I didn't know what all was involved I would be lost, so I can imagine what the jury must be sensing. Worse, the questions have little or no follow-up. It is as if the prosecutor was not prepared for even the answers being given and thus does not know how to probe deeper and make a case. This is bad. This is really bad. Uhhh!"

"Would you say the questioning of Dr. Prolewski was indicative?"

"Of course. After he asked her name and credentials, he asked her to give some testimony on the mother as to her character and the abuse situation that started this whole case. He did not so much as ask whether the mother was capable of making up such a story. Nor did he ask anything about the mother's emotional or mental state after she reported this incident to the good doctor. And instead of going over the time the doctor spent with the mother, so that the jury could understand this woman, the prosecutor suddenly sat down to an audible gasp from the audience. The defense attorney smiled and asked a series of questions about the mother abusing the child in graphic detail, making the mother out to be a really vicious person. The defense attorney further asked whether the mother was known to have a temper and whether or not she was known to swear a lot. And did the mother have an opinion on the defendant, and what that was. With those questions, the mother was clearly shown to be biased against the defendant and would do almost anything to get rid of her. And the prosecutor did not redirect. What was he thinking about? You can't let a jury's opinion about an important prosecution witness in this case be predetermined by the defense attorney. Terrible!"

"In an unusual move, Chief Deputy Charlie O'Shea is holding the child central to this case and is about to take her over to the defendant's desk and point out the defendant Ann Brown. As we have noted before, the prosecution's case has gone badly, either because the prosecutor has not handled the case well or because the defendant's attorney has been very impressive at attacking the evidence. Maybe a bit of both. But outside, analysts have indicated that based on the evidence, this was an open-and-shut case that a prosecutor should have won with ease. Thus, most experts blame the prosecutor for badly handling the case, and the defendant's attorney simply exploited the weaknesses in the prosecutor's case. Any decent defense attorney could have blown this case wide open because of how badly the prosecutor presented the case.

"In any matter, the prosecutor is reaching for a dramatic moment to pull the case back together. He is having the young girl be carried over to the defense's desk to point out the defendant. We can't show her face or any identifying features, but we can focus a bit on the defendant and on the deputy to give you some idea of what is involved here. Let's go inside. You will hear the prosecutor's voice first in the background."

"Okay, can you point to the person who did this to you?" (Pause)

"Your honor, the child is slipping from the deputy's grasp; can you get him to try to hold her in place so she can point?"

"Deputy O'Shea, please try to hold the child in a manner so she can point."

"I am trying, your honor."

"Oh my God."

"No."

"She's pulled the gun from the deputy's holster and as you are watching, she has the gun pointed at Ann Brown. You just heard shots. She has fired point blank at Ann Brown's head. You are seeing confusion in the courtroom. The deputy grabbed the gun from the child. Other deputies have grabbed the child. The defense lawyer is leaning over his client. Parents of the child have run to the child. The judge has just yelled the court to be cleared of all but emergency personnel. We are being driven out of the court, but already medical personnel are beside Ann Brown. The child is being taken away. We have been informed other TV stations are interrupting their regular broadcasts. And we will be feeding to the national networks in just a moment. But from what we have seen, I don't know how Ann Brown could have survived those bullets. And the child was so fast and apparently slippery. I would not be surprised to hear she planned this. As soon as the prosecutor comes out, we will be asking him how this demonstration came about."

"Attorney McMasters has come out of the courtroom. He is our legal advisor for this case. Did you have any idea this was going to happen?"

"Oh my God, no! I was not even aware of the demonstration until the prosecutor asked for it. I could see why he wanted to do something like that, but I was still surprised when it happened. And the gun, my God, my God, who would have thought a child could do that!"

"Hold on. We have just received a flash. The medical examiner has just pronounced Ann Brown dead. We repeat. The medical examiner has just pronounced Ann Brown dead."

Chapter 13

Epilogue by District Judge M. Edward Winthrop

Due to my involvement with the case, I was delegated the task of putting something together to make sense of what happened. I assembled various materials and put them in the order given to this point. I could have handled this as a straight narrative, but I felt the voices were important to be heard. Thus, I organized and edited them appropriately to provide their own consistency. I hope I have been unbiased enough even to present my own involvement properly. That will be for you to decide.

It is also my responsibility to conclude this case. Obviously, the case against the defendant could no longer go forward, so it was dismissed. However, all the evidence will be made public following distribution of this report. On the basis of what the prosecution was presenting to the court, my professional opinion is that a jury would have had a hard time finding the defendant guilty. However, after reading all the other materials, including the defendant's own words, there is no doubt the defendant was guilty.

As for the child, the law is quite clear that someone so young could not be prosecuted. Mental health professionals will be required to meet with the child regularly until she reaches adulthood. It is the hope of the court and everyone associated with the case that the child will as a result turn out to be a responsible, law-abiding citizen in the future, but also one who will be able to get beyond the sexual predatory acts of the defendant. Only time will tell, but the court will be watching.

The agency has undergone a thorough house cleaning. Numerous persons have been removed from their positions. The state, as a result of legislative action, mandated new regulations that hopefully will prevent a similar situation from reoccurring. However, due diligence must be maintained as humanity always has a knack for devising evil and finding ways to inflict evil on people.

The parents and the children are living together. There has been no further abuse of the children.

LaVergne, TN USA
19 February 2010
173528LV00007B/135/P